T0284329

PENGUIN BOOKS
FRAPPÉS FOR THREE

Vidhya Sathyamoorthy is a freelance content writer and blogger. She holds a degree in Business from Monash University Malaysia and a Masters in Economics from University of Malaya. She worked as a corporate trainer and subsequently as a lecturer before discovering her true passion—writing.

Vidhya lives in Kuala Lumpur with her husband and their dog, Patchi. She enjoys writing stories and poems, going on long walks with her dog, and café hopping. *Frappés for Three* is her debut novel, based in part on her own university experience.

Frappés for Three

Vidhya Sathyamoorthy

PENGUIN BOOKS
An imprint of Penguin Random House

PENGUIN BOOKS

USA | Canada | UK | Ireland | Australia
New Zealand | India | South Africa | China | Southeast Asia

Penguin Books is part of the Penguin Random House group of companies
whose addresses can be found at global.penguinrandomhouse.com

Published by Penguin Random House SEA Pte Ltd
9, Changi South Street 3, Level 08-01,
Singapore 486361

Penguin
Random House
SEA

First published in Penguin Books by Penguin Random House SEA 2024

ISBN 9789815144024

Typeset in Garamond by MAP Systems, Bengaluru, India
Printed at Markono Print Media Pte Ltd, Singapore

www.penguin.sg

To Amma and Appa,
who always encouraged me to write

And to my husband, Karthig,
who saw the writer in me long before I ever did

Chapter 1

After what felt like an eternity, the plane landed. The flight was delayed due to bad weather and when it finally reached Subang from Penang, the pilot had to circle the airport, waiting for a runway to clear up.

Maya grew impatient. She had dreamt of this day forever: the day she would leave for college. It was the start of a great new adventure for her. After years of reading about brave, adventurous heroines in books, she was finally going to become the heroine of her own story. Maya Joseph, English literature major, aspiring writer, ready to shake up the literary world! If she ever managed to get off this plane, that is.

Slowly, the passengers disembarked and made their way to the baggage claim area. Maya waited until she saw her purple suitcase with its neon-pink ribbon around the handle— something her mum had added for easy identification. Using all her might, she transferred the massive suitcase onto a trolley. She was tall and slender with virtually no upper-body strength, so this was quite the Herculean feat for her.

As she wheeled the trolley out towards the exit, she thanked her lucky stars that her overstuffed suitcase didn't give way. Maya hailed a cab, and with the driver uncle's help, loaded the unwieldy suitcase into the boot. Soon she was on her way to Maestro University. They drove through Kuala Lumpur and Maya gazed out the window, enjoying the sights of the capital city. Tall skyscrapers, elevated train tracks, huge malls, inviting cafés; they were all calling to her.

Being a Penang girl, Maya was used to the hustle and bustle of city life, but the energy here was different and she loved it. After half an hour or so, the cab driver pulled up in front of the Maestro campus. He helped Maya unload her heavy suitcase, clearly struggling with the sheer weight of it, before closing the boot. Maya paid him with a crisp fifty-ringgit bill, and off he went.

She looked up. On the arch over the impressive gates, the words 'Maestro University' glinted in the sunlight; the words *scinde viam tuam ad gloriam*, Latin for 'carve your own path to glory', inscribed beneath. Maya smiled to herself. She wasn't secretly fluent in Latin or anything; she just had a healthy obsession with all things Maestro. She was definitely ready to carve her own path to glory, but first, how on earth was she going to lug her ginormous suitcase all the way to the dorm?

* * *

Even on wheels, the bag was a nuisance to haul. While Maya was glad that the suitcase and its precious contents were intact, one of the wheels got busted on the way, so she had to half drag, half carry the bag across campus to her dorm. Overall, not a great start to her epic new adventure.

The dorms were pretty modern, much like the rest of the Maestro campus. The dorm building was a tall, condominium-style design with eight rooms in each unit. It was all relatively new, and the furniture was in tip-top condition. Maya's room was on the twenty-second floor. Luckily, the building was equipped with six speedy elevators to cater to early-morning student traffic.

The academic semester didn't start for a few more days, so luckily there were only a few people around to witness Maya's struggle. The open foyer was deserted and so was the library. Two guys were playing frisbee on the field, but they were too invested in the game to notice Maya. After a great deal of difficulty, and a lot of swearing, Maya finally arrived in front of her dorm unit.

This is it. The beginning of the rest of my life. There's no turning back now, she thought to herself. With a mix of excitement and trepidation, she unlocked the front door and stepped inside.

She walked in to find no one in the kitchen or living room. These common areas were at the centre of her dorm unit. The unit then branched out into long hallways, flanked by single rooms on either side.

She wondered what her housemates would be like. She would be living with them for the next three years, so she hoped with all her heart that they were nice, or at least tolerable.

The rooms were numbered from one to eight. According to the email sent by the dorm management, Maya would be occupying Room 6, right next to the kitchen. Maya smiled to herself as she imagined giving out her new correspondence address to friends and family: Room 6, Unit 9, 22nd Floor, Maestro Dorm. The thought of receiving handwritten letters excited the writer in her, but since her contact list consisted mostly of Gen Zers, she wasn't holding her breath.

Maya went into her new room and collapsed on the bed. It had been a tiring journey from Penang to KL. And her heavy suitcase was the final straw that broke the camel's back! As a soon-to-be English literature major, you'd have thought Maya's bags would be full of books. Technically, she did have a lot of books on her, but they weren't really weighing her down. They were all safely tucked away in her Kindle.

Her mum had got her the Kindle for her birthday, and it was easily her most treasured possession. So many hours were spent reading on that thing when she was supposed to be studying, it was a miracle Maya passed her A-Levels. But she wasn't worried about that any more. As an English literature student, she would get to read all the time.

Once she had caught her breath, she sat up with her back against the headboard and opened the Instagram app on her smartphone. She took a selfie and posted a story with the text: *6.1.2017, a day to remember! The start of a new adventure. Wish me luck!*

As she scrolled through her feed, her phone suddenly rang. She answered it, 'Hey, Mum. I just got to my dorm room.'

'I told you to call me when you reached the airport,' retorted Mrs Hillary Joseph in her unique mixed accent. She sounded rather annoyed. Maya's mum and dad had met at university in London many years ago. They fell in love, got married and moved to her dad's home country. Having been in Malaysia for over twenty years, Mrs Joseph's British accent had amalgamated with the local Manglish to create something rather unusual.

'Oh . . . sorry, Mum—'

'It's barely been a day and you've already forgotten your mother!'

'Oh my God, Mum, don't be so dramatic! I haven't forgotten you. I just . . . got distracted, that's all.'

'Distracted doing what? What could be more important than calling your mother?'

'Err . . .' Maya couldn't very well tell her mum that she was scrolling through Instagram. No, she didn't have a death wish, so she chose to stretch the truth just a little. 'One of the wheels on my suitcase got busted, Mum, and I had to half carry, half drag it up to my dorm room. I was just sorting that out.'

'I told your father that that suitcase was no good. He never listens to me, that man.'

Even over the phone, Maya could sense her mum stewing on the other end.

Maya sighed, 'Mum, it doesn't matter. I'm fine. My stuff is all fine. Please just drop it.' The last thing she wanted was to referee a yelling match between her parents over the phone.

'Fine. How was your flight?'

'Awful. The flight was delayed, and the pilot took his own sweet time to land the plane. And there was a screaming baby behind me—'

'I told your father to spring for better seats, but surprise, surprise, he didn't listen—'

'Oh my God, please stop. The flight was fine. Can we just move on?' Maya didn't mean to snap at her mum, but she couldn't conceal her growing frustration. This day was supposed to be about her, not the never-ending drama between her parents. Maya's words were met with a heavy sigh from her mum.

'Things have been a little tense here since you left . . . do you like your dorm room?' Mrs Joseph asked, trying to lighten things up.

'Yeah, it's nice. Anyway, I'd better go and unpack this suitcase from hell. I'll call you later once I'm settled.'

'Okay, honey. Take care. Call me if you need anything. I love you.'

'I love you too, Mum.' Maya lay back in bed wondering how far she would have to travel to escape all her family drama and came to the conclusion that, even if she were on Mars, her parents would find a way to send a communication device up there and drag her into their incessant arguments.

After much procrastination, Maya finally got off her bed and started unpacking. She unzipped her suitcase, which popped open to reveal a mountain of clothes within. Maya was an avid reader, but she was also a teenage girl on the brink of adulthood. She wanted to do this whole university thing in style.

So she had packed virtually every item of clothing she had—jeans, casual tops, pretty blouses, summer dresses, boots, sneakers, and high heels—basically a mini H&M in her suitcase. She had also 'borrowed' a few stylish pieces from her mum's wardrobe. It took her almost two hours to unpack everything. She kept her now empty suitcase on top of her overflowing closet.

All this unpacking had left Maya really hungry. She twisted her long, curly hair into a topknot, grabbed her keys, and headed to the café downstairs. On her way down, the elevator stopped on the seventh floor and a muscular young man, dressed casually in shorts, a sleeveless, white T-shirt, and flip flops walked in. Maya was on her phone, but from the corner of her eye, she noticed Buff Guy looking at her. She glanced up at him. He grinned and winked. Feeling awkward, Maya just looked down at her phone again.

Maya was a beautiful girl. She had smooth, dusky skin and curly hair, which she inherited from her Indian father, Mr Joseph Arumugam, and her Caucasian mother's light-coloured eyes and high cheekbones. Add tall and lean to the equation and Maya

was pretty much an exotic bombshell. However, she had gone
to an all-girls' school for most of her life, so she didn't really
know how to deal with attention from the opposite sex. When
the elevator doors opened on the ground floor, Maya dashed
out of the lift and made her way to the lobby. She was fairly sure
that the email she received had mentioned something about a
café, but she was yet to find her bearings. After walking around
aimlessly for a while, she gave up and approached a security
guard to ask for directions.

'Oh, *studen baru ke*?' the elderly guard asked with a warm,
toothless smile. Maya nodded in response. He then proceeded to
lecture her about university life and the importance of studying
hard in the local Malay language, before giving her directions to
the café. Maya thanked him and hurried along before he could
start lecturing her again.

*Note to self: avoid the sweet, but overly chatty, security guard, especially
when you're late for class!* Maya thought.

The dorm café offered both indoor and outdoor seating.
The seating outside was by the pool. It was a pretty hot day,
so most of the students were sitting inside, enjoying the air-
conditioning and the soft jazz playing in the background. Maya
entered the café and stood in line as she checked the overhead
menu, all the while knowing exactly what she was going to order.

There were two guys waiting in line in front of her. The
first was taking his time, looking at the menu, while the second
was getting impatient. 'Dude, can you move aside? You should
let others go first if you haven't decided what to order!' he said.

The first guy turned around, looking quite shocked. 'Sorry,
I didn't realize there were people behind me,' he apologized.
He stepped aside, letting the second guy order a plate of nasi
goreng, extra *pedas* (spicy). A perfect match for his fiery mood.
Maya went next, ordering a nasi lemak to go. She then stood

aside and waited for her food. After a minute or so, she couldn't help but notice that the first guy still hadn't ordered anything.

He was tall and lean, with messy, black hair. Messy Hair was in faded jeans, a grey T-shirt, and round-framed spectacles. He peered at the overhead menu and Maya could tell that he was pretty confused. 'Hey, do you need help?' she asked.

'Oh, erm . . . yeah, I guess so,' he said awkwardly. 'It's my first day here and I have no idea what to order.'

Based on his accent, Maya guessed he was probably a North Indian. 'Okay, well, what are you into? They seem to have all the usual Malaysian delicacies here: nasi lemak, mee goreng, nasi goreng—'

Maya noticed that Messy Hair was beginning to look confused again. Then, it hit her: of course, he didn't speak Malay. It wasn't just his first day at Maestro, it was probably his first day in Malaysia. The menu must have looked like gibberish to him.

'Do you like noodles or rice?' Maya asked.

'Rice,' he answered immediately.

'Do you like spicy food?'

'Yeah, I do.'

'Go with the nasi lemak. That's what I ordered too. It's always a safe bet.'

'Nasi lemak?' he repeated hesitantly. 'Am I saying it right?'

'Yeah, you're good. Go ahead, place your order.'

'Thanks,' said Messy Hair before turning to order his first taste of Malaysian food. Just then, Maya received her food and waved goodbye to Messy Hair on her way out. She went back upstairs, devoured her nasi lemak and fell asleep reading *Pride and Prejudice* for the gazillionth time on her Kindle.

Chapter 2

On the first day of the semester, Maya woke up buzzing with excitement. She made herself a cup of three-in-one coffee before getting dressed. The first few days were just orientation, but Maya was excited nonetheless. She wore blue jeans, an orange peplum top, and accessorized with some gold bangles. After poking and prodding at her hair, she finally decided to put on a headband before heading out the door.

Over the weekend, she hadn't bumped into any of her housemates. The unit was quiet except for the occasional opening and closing of the front door. Whenever Maya heard the door, she would rush out to greet her housemates and introduce herself, but by the time she came out, they seemed to have disappeared into their respective rooms. Maya wondered whether her unit was haunted, but a quick Google search didn't reveal any frightening horror stories involving their dorm building.

Casting this worry aside, Maya took the elevator down and made her way to the open foyer, where all the new students had been asked to gather. Rows and rows of chairs were arranged facing a makeshift stage with a podium at its centre. Someone was already on the stage giving a speech and Maya hurried to take an empty seat at the back.

'. . . carve your own path to glory. True to our motto, I'm sure every one of you here is bursting with potential . . .' The dean of admissions, Dato' Peter Tan, went on for another twenty minutes, talking about the history and achievements of Maestro—basically a much longer (and more boring) version of the university About Us page.

After that, students were divided into groups of ten and given a campus tour, each group headed by a member of the student council. Maya's group was headed by Jasmine Yeo, a Chinese girl who looked like she had walked straight out of a fashion magazine.

During the tour, Maya tried to socialize with her groupmates. They were pleasant enough, but some of them already had their own cliques and others were conversing with each other in Mandarin, making it difficult for Maya to join in the conversation. The campus tour ended in the open field, where students were asked to regroup according to their respective faculties. Six groups of varying sizes were formed: business, English literature, IT, health science, social science, and engineering.

The business faculty group was by far the largest, with over two hundred students, and Maya's group—the English literature gang—was the smallest, with a measly fifteen students. The student council organized a series of games, including dodgeball, tug-of-war, and the old-school *ibu ayam dan musang* (a Malaysian children's game where one team dodges the attacks of a 'fox' from the opposing team), pitting the different faculties against each other. The business faculty won overall, followed by engineering and then English literature. Maya was proud to be a part of this small but scrappy team of talented individuals.

After the games ended, snacks and refreshments were served at the campus cafeteria, giving the students a chance to mingle. Maya sat down with her English literature gang and enjoyed some mee goreng and teh tarik. She instantly clicked with Esther Cheong, a petite Chinese girl with a black bob and cat-eye spectacles. They connected over their love for the *Hunger Games* series and excitedly discussed their favourite characters in the books.

All her other coursemates were KL natives, who didn't stay on campus like her. As soon as the eating-cum-mingling session came to an end, they hurriedly said their goodbyes as they all wanted to head home before peak-hour traffic. Before parting, Maya and Esther exchanged numbers and saved each other's names with a crossbow emoji at the end.

After bidding farewell to the English literature gang, Maya walked back to the dorm, wishing at least one other person was staying on campus with her. Feeling a little disheartened, she took the elevator up to her dorm unit and opened the front door. Someone was seated at the dining table with her back towards Maya.

For a moment, Maya froze. She had convinced herself that her housemates were all silent ninjas, skilled at the art of swift entry and exit. She contemplated the possibility of the figure before her being a ghost, but then decided not to jump to such ridiculous conclusions.

There's only one way to find out, Maya thought to herself.

'Hi,' said Maya hesitantly as she slowly walked in and shut the front door, trying hard to not turn her back on the unidentified person sitting before her. Although she was fairly sure it wasn't a ghost, she thought it best not to let her guard down.

The girl turned around and, with a mouth full of Maggi noodles, blurted out, 'Oh hey!'

Maya couldn't help but laugh. And that's how she met her best friend, Chong Mei Li.

* * *

Two weeks flew by quickly. Maya enrolled for four classes: contemporary literature, creative writing 101, literature and feminism, and film studies. She signed up for film studies as an elective, thinking it would be fun, but she was wrong. Instead of analysing and discussing movies, the lecturer, Mr Hughes, decided to go for a more theoretical approach.

The recommended text was a five-hundred-page book titled *Breaking Down the Process of Filmmaking*. Mr Hughes followed this text religiously in his lessons, and as much as Maya loved reading, she couldn't get through even two pages of the book without dozing off.

After a particularly dull second lecture, Maya speed walked to her dorm unit to find Mei Li seated at the dining table, eating yet another bowl of Maggi. She had jet-black hair, olive skin, and almond-shaped eyes that were framed by her perfectly shaped eyebrows. Even dressed casually in shorts and a baggy T-shirt, with her hair up in a messy bun, she still looked effortlessly cool and stylish.

'Mei, I've got a huge problem,' said Maya as she collapsed into the chair next to Mei.

'What happened?' Mei mumbled with a mouthful of noodles, her words almost unintelligible.

'I hate film studies! It's so dull. I don't think I can stand a whole semester of this torture.'

Mei swallowed her noodles and said, 'I don't know. Mr Hughes is pretty cute.'

'But his lessons are so boring. Like today, he droned on about this one scene from a super-old, black-and-white movie for over forty-five minutes—and it was a silent film, Mei. A SILENT FILM!'

'Geez. That does sound dull.'

'What am I going to do, Mei? I hate the lectures. I hate the recommended text. I'm going to flunk this class,' Maya cried, burying her face in her hands.

'Why don't you drop the class?' Mei replied calmly.

'What?' Maya looked at Mei hopefully.

'Drop film studies and take up another elective. We have a two-week window to add and drop classes. Easy-peasy.'

'But . . . what class should I take? It's been two weeks. People have already started forming cliques. I'll definitely be an outcast.'

'Well, why don't you take a business class with me?'

Maya pondered on Mei's suggestion. Mei was in her first year like Maya, but she was doing a business degree. Having arrived a little late on campus, she had missed the games on the first day of orientation and the triumphant victory of the business faculty. While joining a class with Mei sounded great, Maya had her reservations. She was an English literature major. Words were her forte, not numbers and graphs. Could she handle a college-level business class?

'You can sign up for my economics 101 class. My lecturer is pretty cool. Plus, I can help bring you up to speed. Econs is my jam,' Mei said excitedly before slurping up the last of her noodles.

Although Maya was hesitant, she had a gut feeling that Mei would have her back. 'All right, Mei, I trust you. I didn't take economics in my A-level, so I'm going to need a lot of help. You up for the challenge?'

'Sure, you can pay me in Maggi packets.'

'Deal!'

Chapter 3

Maya dropped film studies and signed up for economics 101 with Mei. The night before her first econs lecture, Mei gave Maya a crash course on the basics. Using apples as an example, Mei walked Maya through the process of drawing a supply and demand diagram. Mei was a great teacher, and Maya a quick learner; so, after an hour or so, they were done. Maya was now able to draw the diagram with ease, although why the market for apples required such an in-depth analysis was beyond her.

The next day, Maya and Mei walked into the auditorium for their econs 101 lecture. 'Wow! This place is huge,' exclaimed Maya.

'Yeah, close to three hundred students signed up for this class. We've got the biggest venue on campus,' Mei replied.

Maestro University, a relatively new institution, was founded some fifteen years ago. Since then, Maestro churned out numerous graduates who excelled in their respective fields, especially business. Multiple newspaper articles cited Maestro's high-quality teaching staff and its emphasis on industry experience as the reason behind its phenomenal success.

Over the years, Maestro built a reputation as the go-to business school in Malaysia. They received thousands of applications each year, but only took in four hundred of the best applicants. Maestro was less popular for its arts and language programmes, so Maya's English literature classes were all far smaller in size. Maya had applied to other universities, both local and abroad, upon her mother's request, but she had insisted on coming to Maestro for one reason: Susan Tan, her favourite Asian author, had joined the Maestro teaching faculty last year.

Maya and Mei settled down in the middle of the auditorium and pulled out the small, retractable tables attached to the side of their chairs. A few minutes later, Mr Ranjith walked in.

He was a short, stout man with a receding hairline, wearing baggy, black trousers and a maroon shirt with long sleeves, which he had rolled back to his elbows. Although he didn't look like a man who could command a room, much less one filled with three hundred chatty teenagers, the auditorium somehow fell silent when he started talking in his deep baritone.

'All right everyone, settle down. Today, we're going to discuss price control . . .'

Mr Ranjith used slides and a whiteboard to cover the topic. While some may consider price control a rather dull topic, Mr Ranjith brought it to life with his great sense of humour and delivery. After two hours, Maya and Mei walked out of the auditorium along with the other students.

'Babe, I'm so glad I dropped film studies,' said Maya as they walked towards the campus cafeteria for lunch.

'What did I tell you? Mr Ranjith is amazing,' replied Mei.

There were numerous stalls in the cafeteria serving a wide variety of food such as Indian-style mixed rice, goreng-goreng, bread, pastries, wraps, and beverages. Maya bought a plate of mixed rice while Mei ordered a chicken teriyaki wrap before settling down at a table shaded by a large umbrella under the trees. As Maya enjoyed her rice with chicken curry and stir-fried long beans, she looked around at her fellow collegemates.

Most of the tables were occupied by students sitting with their friends, relaxing and laughing boisterously. She could see some students in the distance roller skating and racing one another across the campus. From where they were seated, they had a good view of Maestro's most popular attraction, the rock-climbing wall. Just then, a lanky chap was nearing the top of the wall as his friends cheered him on. Maya couldn't take her eyes off him. She found herself completely invested in this stranger's climb and silently rooted for him. Alas, he hoisted himself up to the top and hit the buzzer. A siren and red lights went off as his friends cheered even louder than before. Everyone in the cafeteria clapped and cheered along. Under one of the nearby trees, a small group had gathered, and they started singing and harmonizing some tunes, acapella style.

Maya couldn't help but feel amazed. Her high school was nothing like this. The students here were so . . . free and uninhibited.

'Maya, this place is really something,' said Mei, reading her mind.

Maya grinned from ear to ear and replied, 'I know, right? I freakin' love it.'

Chapter 4

'With that, we're done with the history of creative writing. Next week, we'll start studying various creative works, starting with my own: *The Dumpling Master's Daughter*. I expect all of you to do your readings before class. Go through the book list I gave you last week and plan your time accordingly. Do this and there's a good chance I'll make decent writers out of you yet. Class dismissed,' said Ms Susan to her tutorial class of eight students.

Dressed in a stylish pencil skirt and silk blouse, Ms Susan flicked her straight, shoulder-length hair before grabbing her designer handbag and sashaying out of class. This class was supposed to end at 4 p.m. and it was now 4.05 p.m. As excited as Maya was to be up close with her hero, she had no time to be starstruck.

She had back-to-back tutorial classes, creative writing followed by econs 101, and she was running late. She stuffed her notebook and other stationery into her backpack, waved goodbye to her classmate, Esther, and practically ran to the Maestro business faculty building. She was panting when she reached the tutorial room and knocked on the door. 'Sorry I'm late, Mr Ranjith,' said Maya. 'My creative writing class ran a little late.'

'That's all right. Come on in and take a seat,' replied Mr Ranjith.

Maya walked in and sat down beside Mei in the third row. The business faculty tutorial rooms were far bigger than the ones over at the arts faculty. Around twenty-four students had signed up for this tutorial class and this room could fit everyone comfortably.

'As I was saying, your first group assignment is due in two weeks. In groups of three, I want you to pick a country and do a ten-minute presentation about the price-control measures implemented in that country. Tell us the effects of those measures, both good and bad, and what you would do differently as policymakers. I'll give you a few minutes to form your groups,' explained Mr Ranjith.

The quiet tutorial room filled with chatter as everyone started forming groups for their first assignment. Maya and Mei didn't know anyone else in the class, so they started talking to people around them. Everyone they asked had already joined another group. Maya was amazed. It had barely been two minutes and people had formed groups at the speed of light.

'Babe, I'm so glad you joined my tutorial class. All these guys seem to be in cliques and these group projects seriously stress me out,' said Mei.

'Hey, at least we have each other. Plus, there are twenty-four students in this class. There's bound to be an odd one out. That person can join us.'

After a few minutes, Mr Ranjith stood up in the front of the classroom and asked, 'All right, have you all formed groups?'

'Yes!' the class chorused in unison.

Maya raised her hand.

'Sir, we're short of one person.'

'Who can join their group?' asked Mr Ranjith. A boy at the back of the classroom raised his hand. 'Okay, you join their group. Problem solved.'

Maya and Mei turned around to see the third member of their group. It took her a while but Maya eventually recognized him. He was Messy Hair. Maya waved at him and he waved back.

'D'you know him?' whispered Mei.

'Sort of. Thanks to me, he now knows the wonders of nasi lemak.'

Mei looked confused, but before Maya could explain, Mr Ranjith started discussing the answers to that week's tutorial questions. During tutorials, he didn't use slides or the whiteboard, except for diagrams, so one just had to listen and write as fast as one could to catch his answers.

After forty minutes of speed writing, Mr Ranjith ended the class. Maya and Mei packed up their things and walked over to the back of the classroom to introduce themselves to Messy Hair.

He was hastily stuffing books into his bag. 'Yeah, I remember you. You're the girl who recommended nasi lemak to me the other day, right? Thanks again, by the way. I really enjoyed it. I'm Rohan.'

'Nice to meet you, Rohan,' said Mei. 'Shall we stay back and discuss the assignment?'

'Er . . . I'm sorry, guys. I can't right now. I've got to go.' Rohan packed up the last of his papers and zipped up his overstuffed bag.

'Oh, that's all right. You stay on campus, right? We do, too. Maybe we can meet up later?' Maya suggested.

'Yeah, sure. Sounds good. See you guys later.' Rohan slung his backpack over his shoulder and rushed out the backdoor.

'Wait, you didn't give us your number,' Mei called out, but he was already gone. Mei sighed and added, 'I think we may have a freeloader in our group.'

'Maybe he has somewhere to be. He stays in the dorm. We're bound to see him around. Don't worry,' Maya replied as she thought about a more pressing matter: what to have for dinner.

Chapter 5

Two weeks later . . .

'Babe, we only have two days left until the presentation,' said Maya in a panic as she burst into Mei's room.

In her usual fashion, Mei was having a bowl of Maggi on her desk while watching a K-drama.

'We've been waiting for Rohan, but he's been a no-show since we met him the other day,' huffed Maya, as she fell onto Mei's bed. 'How did we let so much time just fly by? We're doomed.'

Mei paused the K-drama at what seemed like a pivotal scene. It was going to have to wait. She got up from her desk and flopped down beside Maya. 'Don't be so dramatic. We have no other pressing deadlines for the next two days. If we start now and hustle, we can get it done.'

'What about Rohan?' asked Maya.

'Screw him, lah! He has been MIA for the past two weeks and we have no way of contacting him. We're on our own, babe.'

'Yeah, I guess you're right. Get your things. Let's go down to the café, order a gallon of coffee, and get to work.' With a heavy heart, Mei brought out her bowl of Maggi to the kitchen and dumped the remainder of her noodles into the trash bin. Much like the K-drama, her beloved Maggi was going to have to wait as well.

They headed downstairs and set up camp in a quiet little corner of the café. Luckily, it wasn't very noisy. Most of the patrons either sat outside by the pool, enjoying the cool evening breeze, or opted to *tapau* and enjoy dinner in their rooms instead.

'We've got to choose a country and read up on its price-control measures. Which country should we choose?' asked Maya.

'Shall we just pick Malaysia? We can talk about the maximum prices set for necessities during festive seasons,' suggested Mei.

'That's a good idea, but I think Malaysia is taken, lah. Hold on, let me check.' Maya opened the WhatsApp group for their econs 101 tutorial class on her phone and scrolled through the countries chosen by her other classmates. 'Shoot! Aliya's group has chosen Malaysia already.' Mr Ranjith had been very clear about this. Each group had to choose a different country. He didn't want multiple presentations on the same country.

Choice of country was on a first come, first served basis. Maya and Mei were far from being first, so they had to think of some other country. While they racked their brains over which country to choose, Rohan walked into the café. He didn't see them, or pretended not to, and went straight to the counter to order his food.

'Babe, look who decided to show up,' said Maya. Before Mei could turn around, Maya was already out of her seat and headed towards Rohan, who was looking at the overhead menu. There were a few things in life that made Maya furious. Flaky freeloaders were one of them. 'Hey, Rohan. What the hell?' she said, coming off more aggressive than she had intended.

Rohan turned towards Maya in shock. He initially looked confused, staring at Maya who stood before him with her hands on her hips, knitting his eyebrows, trying to work out what was going on. When it finally dawned on him, his eyes widened and he clapped his hand over his mouth.

'Oh, my God, I'm so sorry, Maya. I totally forgot about the assignment. There were some urgent things I had to deal with this week.'

'Dude, we all have stuff going on! You can't just go AWOL and expect us to do all the work.'

'You're right,' he replied, looking sheepishly at the floor. 'It's not like me to be so irresponsible. I really am sorry, Maya. Things are better now. I'm all yours. How can I help?'

'Order some food and join us over there.'

As Maya walked back to their table, she heard Rohan's order, 'One nasi lemak and three coffees, please.'

Yep, they needed all the caffeine they could get. It was going to be a long night.

* * *

'We could talk about the ration card system in India,' Rohan suggested.

Over coffee, Maya and Mei learned that Rohan was from New Delhi so he was pretty familiar with this system.

Maya scrolled through the WhatsApp group and replied, 'No one has chosen India yet. What do you think, Mei?'

'Let's go for it.'

At 10.08 p.m., Maya typed into the group chat, *Our group is going with India!* and hit send.

'All right, it's official. Rohan, tell us a little about the ration card system, and then we'll read up further online.'

'Sure. Basically, ration cards are issued to low-income families in India. Ration card holders can purchase essential food items at subsidized prices . . .'

For the next two hours, they learned everything they could about this system. Mei focused on the history of ration cards in India while Maya read up about who was eligible for ration cards and what the card holders were entitled to. Rohan, being the one who was most familiar with this system, boned up on the effects of rationing on the Indian economy. Mr Ranjith wanted everyone to cite their sources, so they worked extra hard to find credible sources of information including government websites and news portals.

At midnight, they had to leave the café as it was closing time. They decided to shift to one of the twenty-four-hour study rooms on campus to continue working. As they walked across campus to the business school building, they saw some students chilling in the empty cafeteria, chatting and watching movies on their laptops. They crossed paths with a few other students who were taking a leisurely stroll across campus, sipping on vending machine drinks, chatting and laughing loudly without a care in the world. Maya felt a sudden pang of jealousy. She would give anything to trade the pressures of a nearing deadline for a carefree walk across campus (minus the cheap, but disgusting, vending machine coffee).

It was still early in the semester, so the study rooms were fairly empty. They walked into one on the second floor, switched on the lights and got to work. They discussed the outline of their presentation and started working on the slides.

Rohan, who turned out to be quite the wiz at creating PowerPoint presentations, took over the duty of creating informative yet attractive slides. Instead of huge chunks of text, he broke everything down into brief bullet points and added relevant images. Maya and Mei exchanged glances, both clearly impressed by Rohan's hidden talent.

Halfway through, Mei volunteered to do a coffee run. They downed the bitter vending machine sludge that passed for coffee and kept going. While Rohan continued to work on the slides, Maya and Mei tried to wrap their heads around the concept of APA-style referencing. Gone were the days when they could just cite 'Google' as their source. The girls huddled together and watched a couple of YouTube videos to figure out how to do proper referencing. Maya was baffled at how countless hours had been spent back in high school, learning how to calculate the area of various hypothetical objects, but no time whatsoever had been dedicated to preparing the students for the brutal task of referencing.

At around 3 a.m., Maya tried hard to stifle a yawn and failed. Mei laughed and looked down at her watch.

'Guys, it's getting late. Let's call it a night. We can continue tomorrow.'

They packed up and headed back to the dorm to hit the hay.

Chapter 6

Finally, the day had come.

Maya, Mei, and Rohan had gone through the presentation countless times the night before. They were up first, which made Maya nervous enough, but she also had Ms Susan's class right before and like always, it ran late. As expected, it was 3.59 p.m. and Ms Susan was nowhere near wrapping up the class. She was talking about her trip to China and how it inspired her book, *The Dumpling Master's Daughter*. Hesitantly, Maya raised her hand.

'Ms Susan, I'm so sorry. I've got to go. I have a presentation today at four o'clock,' she voiced out nervously.

Ms Susan looked over at her and waved her hand, gesturing for Maya to go. She then continued with her story.

'All the best, Maya,' Esther whispered as she encouragingly gave Maya two thumbs up.

Maya chucked everything into her bag and ran for it. She was afraid Ms Susan disapproved of her leaving so abruptly, but she couldn't be late. Not after the lecture she gave Rohan the other day. She ran as fast as she could, past the cafeteria and towards the business faculty building. At exactly 4.03 p.m., she arrived at the tutorial room, gasping for air.

Rohan and Mei were at the front of the class, setting up for their presentation. Maya chucked her bag aside and went to stand beside them. Mei was up first, so Maya had a few minutes to catch her breath.

'All right, guys, start whenever you're ready,' said Mr Ranjith from the back of the class. He was seated in the last row, with an evaluation sheet on the table and a pen in his hand.

'Good evening, everyone. Today, we're going to talk about the rationing system in India . . .' started Mei.

* * *

'We believe the rationing system in India has its merits. Although state intervention is often seen as a negative thing, this system gives many low-income households access to affordable food. As policymakers, we would increase supervision for ration shops to ensure that rations are actually being distributed to the people instead of being siphoned off into the black market,' said Rohan, concluding their presentation.

Rohan's closing remark was met with an awkward silence. After a moment or so, he added, 'That's it from us. Thank you.'

Mr Ranjith clapped, nodding his head, and this was followed by a weak applause from their classmates. Rohan made a mental note to include a slide that said 'THE END' in big, bold letters for future presentations.

'All right, good job, guys. To be honest, I was a little worried seeing that you chose your country only two days ago. But overall, it was a very thorough presentation. Well done,' said Mr Ranjith encouragingly.

Maya felt utterly relieved. They returned to their seats and the next group went forward. After all the groups were done with their presentations, Mr Ranjith dismissed the class.

'I'm so glad that went well. Do you guys want to celebrate over dinner? My treat,' said Rohan with a grin on his face.

'Heck, yeah! Let's meet at the café later. Eight o'clock? I really need a nap first!' replied Mei.

* * *

After a well-earned nap, they met up in the café. Maya and Mei ordered mee goreng and Rohan his usual nasi lemak.

'I'm glad that you're enjoying our local nasi lemak, but perhaps it's time to expand the repertoire a little?' said Maya teasingly.

'Oh yeah, I'm practically addicted to it right now. I think you've got to introduce me to other local dishes. What did you guys order? Mee goreng?' asked Rohan curiously.

'Yeah, it's fried noodles, I think you'll like it. The café's mee goreng is pretty good,' said Mei.

The three of them found a table in the corner and settled in. As they ate their dinner, they talked and got to know each other better.

Rohan was a first-year business student like Mei. He was here from Delhi on a scholarship. He wanted to be a teacher, but his parents had encouraged him to take up business and finance for the career prospects as a banker seemed more lucrative. Maya got a sense that money was important in Rohan's family.

She couldn't imagine doing anything other than English literature. It probably wouldn't bring in tons of money unless, by some stroke of luck, she became a bestselling author, but it was her passion. Nobody could talk her out of doing English literature. In fact, her father had tried very hard and failed. Still, Maya couldn't help but feel a great sense of respect for Rohan. He was doing what was best for his family, even if that meant putting his own aspirations aside.

Mei loved fashion and took up business hoping to create her own fashion empire someday. However, her parents, who owned and ran a furniture manufacturing company, wanted her to take over the family business. Mei joked that her interest in furniture lay solely in the size and contents of her wardrobe.

'I want to be a writer,' said Maya when it was her turn to talk about why she joined Maestro. She felt a little embarrassed saying it out loud. As much as Maya loved books, she wasn't convinced that she was a gifted writer. She had her doubts.

'Wow, that's amazing! I'd love to read your work someday,' replied Rohan, encouragingly.

'Oh . . . sure. To be honest, I don't know if it's any good,' Maya muttered, regretting having brought it up in the first place. 'I joined Maestro because of Susan Tan. I'm taking her creative writing class and I'm really nervous about this writing assignment she's given us,' she continued.

'Oh yeah, I know her. She wrote that book, *The Dumpling Master's Daughter*, right?' Rohan asked as he ate his gazillionth plate of nasi lemak with gusto.

'Yeah, that's her most popular work. She's also written a few other books and short stories that I absolutely love. She really has a way with words, and she captures the Asian experience so beautifully.'

'What's the assignment about?'

'Well, I have to write a short story centred around a female protagonist.'

'Why not write about a girl who creates a fashion empire against all odds?' Mei suggested cheekily before slurping up an extra-long noodle.

'It's meant to be a work of fiction, Mei, not a biography. Anyway, I already have an idea. I just have to sit down and write it out.'

They continued talking about the usual stuff new friends talk about: movies, music, food, and travel. Conversation flowed easily between the three of them. Maya's initial impression of Rohan turned out to be way off the mark. He seemed nice, which made her wonder.

After their meal and a round of frappés, she asked, 'Hey, I'm curious. You were MIA for a while then. We didn't see you in class the whole of last week. What happened?'

'Well . . . it's probably easier if I show you. Give me five minutes, then meet me by the pool,' he said before getting up and walking out of the café, leaving the two girls perplexed.

Chapter 7

Maya and Mei waited for Rohan by the pool. After a few minutes, Rohan walked over with an open backpack over his shoulder.

'Hey, thanks for waiting,' he said.

Before he could say anything else, Maya heard a meow and a head popped out of Rohan's bag.

'Is that a kitten?' Mei asked excitedly.

'Yeah. This is Cocoa,' Rohan replied as he put his backpack down and gently lifted the small, brown kitten.

He passed her over to Maya and Mei. Cocoa almost immediately warmed up to the girls, grazing her small furry body against them. She did a small trust fall onto Maya's lap, exposing her belly to the girls and Mei was reminded of Momo, her dog back home. The girls stroked Cocoa and she purred loudly, basking in the attention showered upon her.

As the girls pampered Cocoa, Rohan explained, 'I found her two weeks ago in a drain nearby. Her paw was injured, and she looked pretty ill. I think she had lost her way and couldn't find her mum. So I took her to the nearest vet, but they refused to treat her without payment. I don't have a lot of money on me, so I ended up going to a couple of places before I found someone kind enough to help.'

Maya suddenly felt guilty for letting Rohan pay for dinner.

'Cocoa was pretty sick for a while. The vet said I'd have to keep a close eye on her. I had to give her meds and feed her milk using a dropper every two hours. The other day, when Mr Ranjith gave us the assignment, I was rushing back to check on her. I was only gone for an hour, but she looked awful when I got back to my room. So, I rushed her to the vet again and after that, I didn't dare leave her side. She's starting to get better though. I think the meds are working.'

Maya was speechless. Both she and Mei had been convinced that Rohan was an irresponsible freeloader when, in actual fact, he was a pretty kind and decent guy.

'But that's no excuse. I should've clearly communicated what was going on to you guys, instead of just going MIA like that. I'm really sorry,' Rohan said, looking genuinely remorseful.

'Rohan, please don't apologize. You did a really good thing. I just wish you had told us. We could have helped,' Maya replied.

'Yeah, we love adorable kittens too, you know,' Mei chimed in.

Rohan smiled with relief.

'It's settled then—all three of us are now Cocoa's guardians,' said Maya. 'I have some pocket money saved up so, if she needs more meds or vet visits, I can help.' She caressed Cocoa's head, gazing into her gorgeous, glistening, grey eyes.

* * *

After that, the three of them became the very best of friends. They hung out together after class and took turns looking after Cocoa. Dinner at the dorm café, followed by late-night study sessions and convenience store runs became their regular routine. On weekends, Mei would show Maya and Rohan around KL. Mei grew up in KL before moving to East Malaysia when she was sixteen, so she knew the city pretty well. Rohan was finally leaving his comfort zone of nasi lemak and starting to explore other Malaysian dishes. His new favourites included char kuey teow, prawn mee, and nasi kandar.

Before they knew it, two months had gone by. Maya was in her creative writing 101 tutorial class, nervously waiting for Ms Susan to return their graded assignments.

'Jonathan Liew,' she called out.

A short, plump, bespectacled boy stood up and walked to the front of the class to retrieve his short story. He broke into a wide smile as he looked at his grade and walked back to his seat.

He must have gotten a good grade! Maya thought to herself.

'Maya Joseph,' Ms Susan called out next.

Maya shot out of her seat and hurried to the front. She took her graded assignment and returned to her seat, too nervous to look at her grade. But she had faith in her story. After what seemed like forever, she glanced down at her assignment on the table. To her horror, written across the front in red ink was the dreadful remark: 'Grade: D. Storyline is illogical and writing is simplistic.'

Maya froze. She couldn't believe her eyes. *Illogical? Simplistic? This is what Susan Tan thinks of my work?* Maya thought, mortified.

All her insecurities seemed to have been confirmed through the short and blunt feedback left on her story. Maya blinked, fighting back tears. She couldn't understand how this could happen. Sure, it probably wasn't the greatest short story ever written, but it was something Maya was proud of.

She had written a sci-fi story set in the future in which Earth was no longer habitable and humans were leaving the dying planet for a newly discovered Earth II. Her short story revolved around a group of scientists who had built a time machine to travel back in time and warn the leaders of Earth, in a bid to save their beloved planet from impending doom. Maya had had a hard time deciding how to end her story and had finally gone with:

The six of them got into the time machine and strapped themselves in. The ones who believed in God, or some higher power, prayed for their mission to be successful. Others, including the chief, thought about the way things used to be and what they were fighting for.

The chief closed her eyes, and she was transported back to the farm. Wide open, green meadows filled with grazing cows. The wind in her hair as she galloped around the farm on horseback. Trees and crops as far as the eye could see. The chief's senses seemed to have memorized every square inch of that magical place. The thought of her father's farm, the crops and livestock, being slowly destroyed in this toxic wasteland created by man was too much for her to bear.

None of them knew for sure whether their time machine would work. And even if it did, they had no idea what effects time travel would have on them. But one thing was certain—they had to fight to save their home. Running away wasn't the solution.

At last, the chief pulled the red lever. There was a blinding flash of light . . . and they were gone.

Esther, who was sitting beside her, reached over and squeezed Maya's hand under the table right before Ms Susan called out her name. Hesitantly, Esther went forward to collect her graded assignment. She glanced at her grade and her face fell. Maya immediately knew her friend was in the same boat as her. Esther solemnly returned to her seat and showed Maya her grade. A big, fat 'F' was scrawled across the front page. Esther's eyes brimmed with tears. While Ms Susan carried on with her lesson, Maya squeezed Esther's hand under the table. She looked around to study the class. Over half of her classmates had sullen expressions, probably the result of lower-than-expected grades.

After class, instead of rushing over to the business faculty, Maya, along with Esther, remained seated until all the other students left the classroom. Then they made their way over to the front desk, their graded assignments in hand.

'Ms Susan, can we have a word with you about the assignment?' Maya asked softly.

'Yes, go ahead,' Ms Susan replied briskly as she packed her things.

'I don't understand where I went wrong. I was really excited about this story.'

Ms Susan put her hand out and Maya handed over her story. After a quick glance, Ms Susan said, 'Ah yes, I remember your work. The story doesn't seem very logical. Another planet has been discovered, so why would anyone risk their life going back in time to save Earth? And the open ending leaves the reader wanting.'

'The team didn't want to give up on their home. They felt they owed it to Earth to at least try,' Maya replied, trying to explain herself and her story.

'That's a tad idealistic, don't you think? Plus, the overall writing style is very . . . simple. There's nothing remarkable about it. I mean, it's okay. But I want more than just okay. Talk to Jonathan and have a look at his story. You should aim for that standard of writing next time around,' Ms Susan replied rather

coldly before handing the story back to Maya and gesturing for
Esther to hand over hers.

'Yes, this was the most disappointing one of the lot.
The story is so underwhelming and your tenses are all over
the place. This is not what I was expecting from a student
at the undergraduate level. You really need to buck up and work
hard to improve your writing. Now, if you'll excuse me, I have a
meeting to attend,' she said as she returned Esther's assignment
and walked out of the room, leaving both girls feeling completely
and utterly crushed.

Chapter 8

'Hey, where's Maya?' Rohan asked midway through their economics 101 tutorial class.

'Beats me. Her creative writing class usually runs late, but she should've been here by now,' Mei replied.

Before Rohan could think any further, Mr Ranjith, or Bullet Train as the students now called him, was on to the next question. Rohan and Mei continued writing as fast as they could. After half an hour, their hands felt like they were about to fall off. Luckily, Bullet Train ended the class and put an end to their suffering.

'Rohan, I've got to go. I have an appointment with my marketing lecturer. Call Maya and keep me posted, okay?' said Mei before heading off to the staff room.

Rohan took his phone out of his back pocket and called Maya. There was no answer. He called again only to be greeted by her voicemail.

He texted her: *Hey, you okay? Where are you?*

It wasn't like Maya to miss class like this. She had a thing against skipping classes. She had only missed one class so far that semester and it was because she was running a high temperature. Even then, Rohan and Mei had to force her to stay in her room and rest. Rohan tried calling Maya once more. As the call went to voicemail yet again, Rohan started to get worried. *Maybe she's not feeling well. Maybe she went back to her room,* he thought.

So, Rohan made his way back to the dorm and took the lift up to the twenty-second floor. He walked over to Maya and Mei's unit and rang the doorbell. Betsy, an Australian exchange student, one of Maya and Mei's elusive housemates, answered the door. 'Hi, Betsy. Is Maya in her room?' Rohan asked.

'Hey, hold on. Let me check.'

She walked over to Maya's room and knocked on the door. 'Maya, are you there? Rohan's here to see you.' She knocked again and waited. Finally, she turned around and told Rohan, 'Sorry, I don't think she's in.'

'That's all right. If you see her, could you ask her to call me?'

'Sure.'

As Betsy closed the front door, Rohan thought hard about where Maya could be. Although he considered the whole Find-Your-Friend feature on smartphones a complete invasion of privacy, he couldn't help but feel that it would be pretty handy right now. Rohan decided to call Maya again. Straight to voicemail. 'Where are you, Maya?' he said to himself. And then it hit him. He knew where she was.

But if she was there . . . it meant something was wrong. Rohan made a dash for the elevator. When he got in, he hit the uppermost button and went to the rooftop. The elevator doors opened to reveal a scenic garden area overlooking KL city. Trees and flowering plants were scattered across the rooftop garden with rustic, cobblestone pathways weaving through them.

Maya had first brought Rohan here some time ago, when he had been feeling low and homesick. She had brought him here one evening and they had sat on a bench watching the sunset together. It was hard to be sad in such a beautiful place. The garden, the sunset, Maya and Mei's company—it made him miss home a little less. Since then, whenever any of them had an off day, they would come up to the rooftop and watch the sunset together.

Rohan looked around and found Maya sitting on their usual bench looking into the distance. Cocoa was curled up on her lap, keeping her company.

'Hey, I've been trying to call you,' he said as he approached Maya. Cocoa, startled by this sudden interruption, jumped off Maya's lap disapprovingly. Rohan promptly picked her up before she could stray away, potentially plummeting to her doom.

Maya, who was in a daze, snapped back to reality. She looked over at Rohan and replied, 'Oh . . . sorry. My phone's on silent. I didn't realize you had called.'

'Dude, are you okay? You missed class and we were worried,' Rohan said as he sat down on the bench beside Maya, carefully placing Cocoa next to him, where she proceeded to cosily curl up once again.

Maya reached into her backpack and took out her story. She passed it over to Rohan. He saw the grade and feedback in red ink right on top. *Damn! Susan is harsh*, he thought to himself.

'Did you ask her what she meant by this?'

'Yeah. She said it was "okay". Not remarkable. Just okay.'

Maya's eyes started to well up. As tears streamed down her face, Maya turned away. She was embarrassed to face Rohan. She had once told him that she wanted to be a writer. That was before she realized she lacked any sort of talent.

'Is that all she said?'

'She said my story didn't make sense, the ending left readers wanting, and . . . my writing is too simple.'

They sat in silence as Rohan started reading Maya's story. As he got to the end, he couldn't help but smile.

'Maya, this is good! I love all things sci-fi, and I enjoyed reading this. It kept me hooked right to the end.'

'Really?' asked Maya in disbelief.

'Yes, really. For what it's worth, I think the ending is perfect. The story is about fighting for what you love, even when the odds are stacked against you. Whether they succeed is secondary. The open ending kind of makes me think, would I have done the same, not knowing how things work out at the end? And that's what stories should do, Maya. They should challenge you and make you think about stuff. Maybe the dumpling man's daughter doesn't appreciate open endings, but I do.'

As sucky as Maya was feeling, she couldn't help but laugh a little. 'It's the *Dumpling Master's Daughter*,' she corrected. Maya pointed at the negative feedback scrawled over her story and added, 'I appreciate your being so kind, Rohan, but you don't understand. Susan Tan hated my story. And what's worse, I actually thought it was good.'

'It *is* good, Maya. This is just one person's opinion.'

'Yeah, one very important person's opinion!'

'Says who? Sure, she's an established author, but that doesn't mean she's always right. I know she's your hero and all, but the fact is, she's not qualified to teach. She's not guiding you properly. A good teacher would recognize that every story deserves to be told and would guide you to tell that story in an authentic way.'

'I don't think you're being fair—' Maya began but Rohan cut her off.

'I don't care about being fair. Susan didn't like your story. But I did. I'm not just saying this because I'm your friend. I wouldn't do you that disservice. I genuinely like your story. As a writer, you need to remember that some people will like your work and some people won't. And that's okay. You don't have to please everyone.'

'I don't know if I'm meant to be a writer, Rohan.'

'Of course, you are. Maya, the reason you're upset is because being a good writer means everything to you. Right now, at this very moment, I can see, as clear as day, that this is what you're meant to do. Is this a good story? Yeah! Is this the best story you'll ever write? No. With every story you write, you're only going to get better, Maya. You can't give up now. You have to keep going. Promise me that you'll keep writing.'

Rohan extended his pinkie to Maya. She smiled and curled her pinky around his. Cocoa purred, as if in agreement.

'Okay . . . I promise.'

'Good.'

The sun was setting in the distance. They sat in silence, looking at the city beyond, admiring the different shades of orange and pink that painted the setting sky. After some time, Maya called out, 'Rohan?'

'Yeah?'

'Thank you.'

'Any time.'

Chapter 9

The rest of the semester flew by. Mei, who met with her lecturer to discuss how she could combine her love for fashion with the marketing knowledge she learned in class, started 'Totally Mei'—an Instagram business account to market her looks and styling skills. Her lecturer advised her that this would be a great way to build an audience that she could later leverage when she starts out in the fashion industry. Mei posted everyday looks jazzed up with affordable accessories and thrift store finds. In a little over three months, Mei's follower count grew to an impressive 4,500.

Maya, of course, spent most of her time writing stories. She wasn't sure whether Rohan was right about Ms Susan, so she decided to submit her stories wherever she could: magazines, newspapers, and writing competitions. Most recently, Maya submitted a story about a young Indian girl joining a Chinese vernacular school to a national-level story writing competition. Deep down she felt she wouldn't win, but she had to try anyway. Maya knew she shouldn't seek external validation, but she was a young writer, and she really didn't know if she was any good. Was Ms Susan's feedback a matter of one person's personal opinion or was it a fact? By hook or by crook she had to find out.

Meanwhile, Rohan was tutoring O-Level students online to earn some extra cash. While his scholarship covered the tuition and dorm fees, the monthly allowance he was given was a rather small sum. He felt bad asking his parents for money when they had his three younger siblings to worry about, so he brushed up on his O-Level economics and business studies and started tutoring online for US$15 per hour. With just under a month until the end of the semester, Rohan was excited to go home for the semester break. It was a relatively long summer break, and he couldn't wait to go back to Delhi and see his family. This was the first time he'd been away from home for so long and he was dreadfully homesick.

After a rather frustrating tutoring session with a bright, but lazy, teenage boy from Australia, Rohan was lying in bed, listening to some Bollywood tunes when he heard the upbeat Skype ringtone. He smiled to himself as he sprang out of bed and sat at his desk. It was old-fashioned, but Rohan's dad was used to Skype and he didn't like change. Rohan answered the call excitedly, eager to catch up with his parents and sisters.

'Hi, Mummy! Hi, Papa,' Rohan waved enthusiastically to greet his parents who appeared on the screen.

Mr and Mrs Das were seated beside each other, facing their webcam. As a middle-class Indian family, they had a single family computer that everyone shared. It was a somewhat bulky, outdated model, but Mr Das had managed to get a good deal on it. It came with an external webcam that was clipped on top of the computer's monitor.

'Hi, *beta*, can you hear us?' the plump Mrs Das, wearing a red salwar suit, practically shouted as she leaned closer to the webcam to speak.

Rohan smiled to himself. 'Yes, Mummy. Don't worry, I can hear you. How is everybody?'

'All are good here, beta. How are your studies coming along?' Mr Das asked with a rather stern expression. Although Mr Das had a reputation as a funny man among his friends, he was always quite strict when it came to matters relating to academics.

'It's going good, Papa. The finals are coming up soon and I'm confident I'll do all right,' Rohan lied, hoping that he sounded convincing.

The truth was, the syllabus covered in Maestro was pretty challenging. He was able to wrap his head around most of the topics that were taught in his classes, but he wasn't very confident about the exams. At any rate, he didn't think it wise to share this bit of information with his father.

'You must strive to do better than just all right, beta. I know people always say the first year is the honeymoon phase, but there's no such thing. You must work hard from the get-go and maintain your CGPA if you want to land a good job here once you graduate,' Mr Das replied, clearly not satisfied with his son's answer.

'How would you know? It's not like you went to university,' Mrs Das chimed in sassily before adding, 'Beta, you look so thin. Are you eating properly? Do they have proper food for you all over there?'

Although his father's insinuations stung, Rohan decided to let it go. There was no point in having an argument over Skype.

The connection was far too choppy to get his point across. Instead, he decided to lighten the mood. 'Mummy, I've always been thin. Stop worrying about me; the food over here is great. I'm eating well, actually,' he replied before adding, 'but I miss your cooking, Mummy. The chapatis over here are nowhere near as good as yours. I can't wait to come home soon.'

At the mention of Rohan coming home, his parents exchanged looks.

'Beta, about that . . . we checked the flight prices online and they're quite expensive. It's probably due to the school holidays. So, Mummy and I were thinking . . . maybe you can come home for the next semester break instead. We can book the ticket early to get a better deal.'

'Oh . . .' Rohan's heart sank.

'Of course, we want you to come home, but everything is so expensive nowadays. The price of onions has gone up by twenty rupees a kilo. And bhindi, even more. Your scholarship covers the dorm fees even during semester break, right, beta?' Mrs Das inquired.

'Yes, Mummy.'

Rohan tried hard to conceal his deep disappointment. He desperately wanted to go home, especially with his birthday coming up, but his parents had a lot of financial commitments, including school fees for his three younger sisters, and he didn't want to make them feel bad.

'I wish you had listened to us and gone to university here in Delhi, beta. Then I wouldn't have to be separated from my only son,' Mrs Das said emotionally, using the dupatta of her salwar to dab her eyes.

Rohan had to be strong. This wasn't the time to throw a tantrum to get his way. He had made his bed and now he needed to lie in it. 'Mummy, I'll be back before you know it.

Six months is nothing; it'll fly by just like that. And we can still see each other on Skype,' Rohan replied, putting on a brave face for his parents.

He was about to inquire about his sisters when the connection became unstable. The video began to lag and the audio turned choppy. It became hard to make out what his parents were saying.

'Okay, beta . . . poor connection . . . call you this weekend . . . eat properly . . . take care . . .' Rohan waved at the screen and ended the call. He shut his laptop and sat numbly at his desk, staring at nothing in particular, before heading downstairs to grab dinner with his friends.

* * *

With their final exams approaching, the three of them put everything else aside and focused on revising for the exams. They were given a two-week study break before the finals, and they basically set up camp in one of the campus study rooms. Studying from 8 a.m. right up to midnight, taking breaks in between for meals and to feed Cocoa, became their new routine. During their long study sessions, they took turns getting vending machine coffee for each other. That stuff was gross, but it was cheap and it got the job done. Although it was tiring, Maya enjoyed the company of her two best friends.

In the second week of their study break, Maya received an email from Ms Susan that made her heart skip a beat.

Maya,
Meet me in my office today at 3 p.m.
Susan

So, after a late lunch, she reluctantly made her way to Ms Susan's office. She wasn't quite sure why Ms Susan wanted to meet her, but she had a bad feeling about it. As her mind anxiously raced through one worst-case scenario after another, she wrapped her arms around herself and trudged along, wishing her mum was there to offer a warm, comforting embrace. The final grade for creative writing 101 was purely based on assignments. There were no final exams for this subject. The course consisted of five assignments in total. Maya's grades improved after her first story, but she never made it beyond a 'C+'. Finally, Maya knocked hesitantly on Ms Susan's door.

'Ah yes, come in, Maya. Have a seat,' Ms Susan said, barely shifting her gaze away from her computer screen.

Maya walked in awkwardly and sat across the desk from Ms Susan as she continued to stare intently at her screen. A few months ago, Maya would have given anything to have this kind of one-on-one time with her hero, but after her first semester in Maestro, she understood why people often advise against meeting one's heroes.

'You wanted to see me?' Maya asked nervously.

Ms Susan nodded, paused what she was doing, and turned to look at Maya with a stern expression. 'Yes. I'll cut to the chase—it's about your grade.'

'Oh . . . what's wrong?'

'Well, you're on the verge of failing and I can't decide whether or not to pass you. Your string of Ds and Cs have resulted in a disappointing final grade.'

Maya could feel her heartbeat speeding up. Her palms grew clammy and her mind raced. She knew she wasn't doing great, but she thought she would at least pass the class.

'Maya, I have to ask: Why did you take up creative writing?'

'I . . . I want to be a writer,' Maya managed to spit out through the anxiety she was experiencing.

Ms Susan let out a derisive laugh before replying, 'Maya, I'm going to be honest with you. You're not suited to be a writer. I advise you to cut your losses and drop writing. Take up something else.'

Maya couldn't believe her ears. Rohan was right. Not about Maya being a good writer (she still wasn't convinced about that), but about Susan freakin' Tan not being qualified to teach. As Susan tactlessly turned back towards her computer screen, Maya took a moment to compose herself.

Finally, she said, 'With all due respect, Ms Susan, I disagree. I may not be a great writer, but I love writing stories. With time, I know I'll grow and get better.'

'Over the last six months, I can't say I've noticed much improvement,' Susan replied crassly.

Maya winced at those hurtful words. She tried hard to fight back her tears. 'I'm sorry you feel that way. I've done my best to improve, based on limited and vague feedback. I didn't mean to disappoint you.'

Susan shot her a glare and snapped, 'Fine. I'll pass you. Not because you're a decent writer, but because I don't want you in my class again next semester. I prefer not to waste my time. Shut the door on your way out.'

'Thank you for your time, Ms Susan,' Maya replied before leaving the office with her head held high.

Chapter 10

Maya didn't tell Rohan and Mei about what had actually happened with Susan. They were stressed out about the exams already and the last thing Maya wanted to do was distract them. As hurtful as Susan's words were, Maya tried hard to forget about the incident. *At least I'll pass*, she consoled herself. Now, she had to focus on her other three subjects: contemporary literature, literature and feminism, and economics 101.

She revised economics 101 with Rohan and Mei. Mr Ranjith told the class that the exam would be a mix of multiple-choice, short-answer, and essay questions. The three of them went through past year papers together and brushed up on all the important diagrams. For her other two subjects, the final exams would consist of only essay questions. Maya wasn't quite sure how to prepare for that, so she focused on going through the key texts again.

Finally, after a lot of hard work and stress, finals week started. Maya's English literature papers were up first. They were back-to-back on the same day. Apart from her hand throbbing from so much writing, Maya felt good about those papers. Two days later, they sat for the economics 101 exam. The paper was challenging, but not overly so. Going through multiple past year papers really paid off. Maya, Rohan, and Mei were sure they would pass at the very least. After that paper, Maya was free. Rohan and Mei had another three days of torture before they were done. Maya's flight back to Penang for the semester break wasn't until the following week, so she kicked back and enjoyed her newly earned freedom in her dorm room, catching up on lost sleep.

As soon as Rohan and Mei completed their final paper, the three of them went out to celebrate. Maya invited Esther to join in their post-exam hangout. The gang went to a nearby eatery called Paradise Café for brunch. They ordered pizzas, nachos, truffle fries, and lattes. Since it was a working day, the café was fairly empty. They spent the rest of the afternoon there, chatting and unwinding after a stressful month. Maya eventually told them about what had happened with Susan.

'She's such a bitch!' exclaimed Mei.

'Yeah, she's the worst,' Esther agreed, glumly.

Maya shrugged. She had made peace with what had happened. 'I guess not everyone is going to like my writing, and that's okay,' she said as she glanced at Rohan.

Rohan smiled and replied, 'Well, we love your writing. Just don't forget us when you're a famous writer one day.'

'If I ever become a published author, I'll dedicate my first book to you guys! Happy?' she quipped.

'Fine by me!' Mei replied. They laughed and ordered another round of lattes. After a few hours, they split the bill and then decided to head back to campus. They booked a Grab, and all the way back to their dorms, Rohan and Mei argued about vampire fashion. Rohan believed that vampires didn't care about fashion, but Mei vehemently opposed this argument, citing the gorgeous vampires in *Twilight* as evidence.

While Maya laughed at their antics, she couldn't help but notice that Esther was particularly quiet. She had barely said anything in the café, quietly sipping her coffee as the three of them chattered boisterously, revelling in post-exam bliss. Even in the Grab car, Esther just leaned back and stared out the window, not saying much really.

The car finally pulled up in front of Maestro. Rohan and Mei got down and started making their way towards the dorm, all the while still arguing passionately. Maya and Esther walked at a slower pace behind them.

Once Rohan and Mei were out of earshot, Maya asked, 'Esther, are you okay? You've been super quiet all day.'

Esther turned to look at Maya, her eyes brimming with tears. 'Maya, I have something I need to tell you.'

Maya got a sense that this was a private matter, so she called out to her friends to go ahead without her. Hesitantly, Rohan and Mei waved at them and then forged ahead towards the dorm. Maya led Esther towards the deserted campus cafeteria, and they sat down at their usual table under a tree.

'What's wrong, Esther? Are you okay?'

'No, I'm not okay. Nothing is okay,' Esther replied, before bursting into tears.

Maya put her arms around Esther's shoulders comfortingly. She extracted a pack of tissues from her sling bag and offered it to Esther. After a few minutes, Esther had no more tears left to cry.

'Tell me, Esther. What's wrong?'

'I won't be able to continue my studies here in Maestro next semester. I'm transferring to a different university,' Esther replied before blowing her nose into a tissue.

'WHAT?!' Maya exclaimed in shock.

'Before our exams, Susan called me into her office as well. She told me that I had failed her class and that it was pointless to sign up for it again next semester.'

'Esther, she's just a big bully, you don't have to leave—'

'I don't have a choice, Maya. Creative writing 101 is a prerequisite subject for our programme and as long as Susan teaches the subject, there's no way I'll pass. I spoke to my parents, and . . . I'm switching to a business programme.'

'But you love to write! There must be something we can do, Esther.'

Esther smiled weakly. 'It's sweet you think that, but there's nothing we can do.'

'Well . . . you don't have to leave. If you want to switch to business, you can stay right here in Maestro. They have a great business programme. Plus, Rohan and Mei can show you the ropes,' Maya pleaded desperately.

'The business programme here is very competitive, Maya. I applied for an internal transfer but got rejected.'

'Why didn't you tell me any of this, Esther? You didn't have to go through it all alone.'

'I was holding on to that last bit of hope that I can stay here with you guys. I didn't want to bum you out until I knew for sure.'

Without realizing it, tears had started flowing down Maya's cheeks. 'Where will you go?'

'I'm transferring over to Maestro's sister university in Cyberjaya. I flunked creative writing, but if I pass my other papers, I can transfer the credits over there.' The two of them sat in silence, watching as a few students scaled the rock climbing wall nearby. 'I'm going to miss you, Maya.'

Maya turned to Esther with steely determination. 'No, we're not doing this. We're not doing soppy goodbyes. That would mean admitting we're leaving each other's lives for good, which we're not. Cyberjaya isn't that far away. We can always meet and catch up on weekends. And more importantly, you can still write. Don't you dare think of giving up. Your stories are lovely, Esther.'

Esther leaned in and hugged Maya. 'That means a lot.' Despite Maya's stout refusal to engage in an emotional farewell, she returned Esther's embrace.

'Okay, next order of business. We talked about doing it in our final semester, well, screw that! Let's do it now. You're not leaving until we do this.'

Esther smiled knowingly and replied, 'I'm down if you are.'

'Oh, I'm down, baby,' Maya replied cheekily before springing out of her seat in excitement. 'Let's go!'

* * *

'Come on, Esther. You're almost there, you can do it,' Maya cheered as Esther passed the halfway mark. Maya took her job as Esther's belayer very seriously. With diligent adjustments, she made sure the rope wasn't too tight or too lax. The last thing she wanted was for Esther to fall and injure herself on her last day.

Esther started off quite shaky, but once she got the hang of things, she grew more confident scaling the wall. She even began to see the appeal of this daunting, yet satisfying, sport. She lifted one leg up into a groove and when she felt stable, she lifted herself up and grabbed on to one of the protruding rocks before eyeing her next possible step. It was exhilarating! For a moment, she forgot all about her woes, leaving Maestro and

Maya, starting from scratch in a new, unknown place. At that moment, it was just her and the wall before her that she needed to conquer.

'This really her first time, ah?' the wall climbing operator, Chandran, asked curiously as he looked up at Esther, clearly impressed.

'Yeah, I guess she's a natural,' Maya replied, wishing she had gone up first. She was definitely the opposite of a 'natural' and was going to look like a hot mess in contrast. Soon after, Esther reached the top and hit the celebratory buzzer. In the usual fashion, red lights and a siren went off. Maya cheered loudly, forgetting her belaying duties for a moment, but soon regained her composure when Chandran cleared his throat warningly. Esther swung down stylishly like she'd been doing it all her life. Maya just stared at her wide-eyed in admiration.

'Babe, that was freakin' amazing,' Maya gushed as Esther removed her harness.

'Beginner's luck, I guess,' Esther shrugged, her cheeks slowly turning red. 'I'm sure you'll do even better. Come on, let's get you hooked up.'

A few minutes later, it was Maya's turn to scale the formidable wall. The two of them had made a pact of sorts to climb this wall together after one of their creative writing lectures. They had been walking towards the cafeteria to get a drink after a rather glum class with Susan Tan when they heard the distinct sound of the siren. A girl Maya recognized from orientation looked over the moon at the top of the wall. There was something about the look on her face that kind of stuck with Maya. It was the sheer unadulterated joy and pride at having accomplished something that had once seemed impossible.

'We're going to get through this. If that four-foot-nine girl can conquer that wall, there's no reason why we can't conquer this whole undergrad thing. I know it seems impossible now, but we can do it, Esther. And when we do, we're going to climb that wall and slam that annoying-as-hell buzzer,' Maya recalled saying to Esther passionately.

Without questioning her logic or reasoning, Esther had agreed, and they had sealed the deal with a pinky promise, so it was as good as a legally binding contract. Months later, Maya was kicking herself for making that promise. She had a mild (but very real) fear of heights and instantly regretted her life choices the moment she stood face-to-face with the wall.

She mimicked Esther's movements the best she could. Find a groove, lift a leg, hoist oneself up, and repeat. Slowly but surely, she reached the halfway mark.

'You're doing great, Maya,' Esther said, encouragingly.

Maya then made the mistake of looking down. She instantly froze and clung to the wall for dear life. 'Oh gosh, this is higher than I expected . . . I don't think I'm going to make it to the top.'

She screwed her eyes shut and took a few deep breaths. She managed to calm down a little, but when she opened her eyes, she discovered she was still terrified of heights and so she continued to cling to the wall helplessly.

'Maya, you can do this, you're already halfway there. You're not going to fall, I've got you,' Esther urged from down below.

With her eyes closed, Maya nodded and took a few more deep breaths. When she opened her eyes, she was still afraid, but she knew she could rely on Esther. Without looking down, she put one foot above the other and made her way gingerly to the top. With one final push, she hoisted herself up and hit the buzzer. Maya never thought she would ever be so grateful to hear the sound of that annoying siren.

'I did it!' Maya screamed excitedly.

'Yes, yes, now come down before you hurt yourself,' Chandran replied dourly. 'I've seen snails move faster than this one,' he muttered under his breath.

Cautiously, Maya swung back down. As soon as she reached the ground, Esther threw her arms around Maya. 'You got to the top. I knew you could do it!'

'I didn't think I was going to make it, babe. Did I forget to mention I was scared of heights?' Maya replied returning Esther's embrace in an emotional moment.

Esther chuckled. 'Seems like something you might want to mention before climbing a twelve-foot wall.'

'Okay, girls, your hour is up. Return your gear and sign out,' a bored-looking Chandran said as he turned and walked away to the small office nearby.

'I imagined us doing this in our final year. I can't believe this is all happening so fast,' Esther said as the adrenaline rush settled down and reality kicked in again.

'Don't worry, we can find new things to do together. Who knows? There might be a better wall to climb on your new campus,' Maya replied as she removed her harness.

'You'd be willing to climb another wall with me?' Esther teased.

'Hell no! I can't take this kind of stress. I'll be a supportive bystander next time.'

They returned the gear, and hand in hand, they walked into the sunset (or more accurately, towards the car park where Esther had parked her Myvi). They hugged each other once again and said goodbye. As Esther drove away from Maestro University, Maya was left standing alone by the kerb. It was a sad moment, but she was confident that Esther would thrive wherever she went and that they would continue to be friends long into the future.

With a heavy heart, Maya made her way back to the dorm.

Chapter 11

The day before Maya and Mei flew home, the three musketeers had to do something they were really dreading. Maya woke up that morning feeling utterly awful. She dragged herself out of bed and got ready before heading down to the dorm café. Mei and Rohan were already there with Cocoa sleeping soundly in her crate on the floor. They ordered some sandwiches for breakfast and ate them in a gloomy silence.

Finally, Maya voiced out what everyone was brooding over: 'Do we have to do this? Can't we just tell them that we changed our minds? I'm sure it happens all the time. We'll just hide her, no one will know.'

Rohan sighed. 'I don't want to do this either, but we have no choice.'

'I know it sucks, but we can't keep Cocoa. You read the e-mail the stupid dorm management sent out. "No pets allowed."

If we're caught, they'll fine us 500 Ringgit. They're crazy! Where will we get that kind of money?' Mei replied in exasperation as she bent down to check on Cocoa. Still fast asleep.

Reluctantly, Maya admitted defeat. 'I'm going to miss her.'

'Me, too. It's going to be weird, not having her around,' Mei said, looking up at the ceiling in a bid to hold back her tears.

'Rohan . . . are you sure we can trust these people?'

'Well, they seem nice. The family has two other cats, so Cocoa won't be alone.'

Once they finished their sandwiches, they took a Grab car to the meet-up point. Rohan carried Cocoa's crate on his lap, and they could hear her purring inside.

'I hope she likes her new family,' Mei said softly as she looked out the window.

'I have a feeling she will,' Rohan replied, looking at Cocoa affectionately.

The Grab driver turned into a housing area in Petaling Jaya and dropped them off in front of house number thirty-seven. Maya rang the doorbell and a plump Malay woman, Kak Lina, opened the door and greeted them cheerily.

'Hi, you must be Rohan. Come, come inside. My children are very excited to meet Cocoa. They'll be home soon.'

Awkwardly, they went in, not knowing what to expect. The living room felt a little dated, but cosy. Rattan chairs were arranged around a wooden coffee table covered with a lace tablecloth. In the corner stood a bookshelf that held storybooks and academic workbooks for various age groups. The walls were filled with decorative artwork and framed family photographs.

'Please sit. Make yourselves at home,' Kak Lina said.

They sat down on the rattan chairs and Rohan placed the crate gently on the floor and undid the latch. Cocoa emerged, stretched, and began exploring her new home. Soon after, two other cats strolled in from the kitchen. One was a rather large, black female cat with white streaks and the other was a smaller, ginger tabby. The two cats stopped in their tracks when they saw Cocoa, probably surprised to see another feline in their territory. Cocoa, with her usual charm, approached them slowly and before long, they were meowing and licking each other.

'Wow, your Cocoa is so friendly,' Kak Lina sounded very impressed.

'Yes, she's a sweetheart,' said Mei, beaming like a proud mama.

Despite their protests, Kak Lina insisted on serving them cold lemonade and an assortment of kueh, 'You've come all the way here to drop off Cocoa. At least have something, lah.' They were still chatting over kueh, when Kak Lina's children came home from school. The three young boys, clad in primary school uniforms and backpacks, shrieked in joy at the eagerly anticipated arrival of their new furry friend.

The children played with Cocoa excitedly and the three musketeers joined in. The cats leapt from person to person, enjoying all the attention being bestowed on them. Whenever the children grew overexcited, Kak Lina would remind them to be gentle, which Maya really appreciated. What was supposed to be a quick drop-off turned into a two-hour meet-and-greet session with Kak Lina's family.

At half past two, they decided not to overstay their welcome and bid farewell to Kak Lina, her kids, and, of course, dear Cocoa. Maya scooped Cocoa into her arms and looked into her glistening, grey eyes. She remembered the first time she had looked into those lovely eyes when they sat by the pool months ago. Up until then, she hadn't believed in love at first sight, but the instant she'd held Cocoa, she had known she would do whatever it took to keep her safe. Maya's vision got blurry as tears filled her eyes.

Yet another goodbye, she thought to herself. As her tears overflowed down her cheeks, Cocoa raised her tiny head and licked Maya's face. She couldn't help but chuckle.

'I'm going to miss you too, buddy.'

'Don't be sad, dear. You are always welcome to visit Cocoa whenever you want,' said Kak Lina.

'Thank you, Kak Lina.'

After a tearful farewell, they left to begin their semester break, taking comfort in the fact that Cocoa was now home.

Chapter 12

After a long flight, Mei was finally back in Sabah. She hailed a cab from the airport to take her home. Her family stayed in a double-storeyed, terraced house in a quiet, suburban area in the capital city of Kota Kinabalu. The cab pulled up in front of her house and before Mei could even open the front gate, Momo, her family dog, dashed out to greet her. Momo was a medium-sized Malaysian mongrel with short, dark brown fur. Her tail was wagging at top speed as she excitedly waited for Mei to enter the front yard.

As soon as she did, Momo started jumping exuberantly in circles around Mei. Mei bent down to greet her furry friend and Momo took this opportunity to give Mei big, sloppy kisses.

'I'm happy to see you too, Momo.'

Mei entered her home, Momo leading the way, and was greeted by her family: her parents and younger sister, Sue (short

for Chong Sue San). After hugs and kisses were exchanged, Mei
went up to her room to freshen up. Momo tailed Mei up to her
room, afraid that her human friend would disappear again when
she wasn't looking.

While the rest of the house was furnished with antique
mahogany furniture (products of their family's furniture
business), Mei's room was filled with edgy second-hand furniture
that she had sourced from various places online. Despite her
parents' protests, Mei had insisted on decorating her room
herself, with bold colours and pieces to reflect her personality.

Mei washed up and headed back down to have lunch with
her family. Her mum had prepared a welcome home meal
consisting of rice, lemon chicken, kam heong lala, bak choy,
and mixed vegetables. Mei took some chicken and bak choy,
avoiding the lala altogether. Mei wasn't a fan of shellfish, but
her mum always made either lala or prawns for special family
meals because they were her sister's favourites. Mei didn't really
mind, but she had been hoping to have some of her mum's
delicious braised pork belly. She had been craving it all through
the semester.

It's okay. I'll ask Mama if we can make it together later, Mei
consoled herself.

'Mei, you so skinny already. Spending all your pocket money
on clothes, ah? You need to eat more,' her mum said as she piled
lala onto Mei's plate.

'Er . . . thanks,' Mei replied. When her mum wasn't looking,
Mei discreetly fed the lala to Momo under the table.

Over the next few days, Mei helped her parents with the
administrative work for their family business. The Chong
family operated one of the largest furniture manufacturing and
distribution companies in East Malaysia. Mei had been helping

them with paperwork and accounting since high school. As the eldest child, she was expected to do her part to keep the show on the road. Her younger sister, Sue, only two years her junior, had somehow managed to avoid shouldering any responsibility.

'Aya, you know Sue, lah. She's very young and playful. Just let her do what she wants, lah,' her mum would always say when Mei brought up the issue of Sue pitching in as well.

Mei felt guilty to admit it, but part of the reason she had applied to Maestro instead of the local universities in Sabah was to escape the pressure of eventually taking over the family business. Mei had lost count of the number of times she had told her parents that she was interested in fashion.

'You can wear whatever you want. Fashion can be your passion, your hobby. It's not going to put food on the table,' had been her dad's usual answer.

This time, however, Mei was determined to get her point across. Sue was out with her friends and over dinner, Mei brought up the taboo topic once again.

'Papa, I want to show you something.' Mei whipped out her phone, opened her 'Totally Mei' Instagram page, and handed it over to her dad. Mr Chong took his daughter's phone and put on his glasses before peering at the screen.

'What is this? Social media, ah?'

'Yeah, it's Instagram. See this number on top? That's my follower count. I set up this page to share looks and styling tips. Close to 5,000 people follow me. A couple of local brands have even approached me for sponsorship deals.'

Mr Chong, an avid mahjong player, was renowned for his poker face. But, however good his expressionless face was for mahjong, it was not so good when dealing with teenage daughters. He scrolled down and replied, 'Aya, why need to wear such short skirts? Hello, you are studying business, not going for fashion show.'

Although his words stung, Mei knew this wasn't going to be an easy battle to win. 'Actually, it was my marketing lecturer who suggested that I create an Instagram fashion account. It's not just about dressing up and taking pictures, you know, there's a lot of marketing know-how and strategies that go into it. Social media is the future of business.'

'Social media can get likes and followers, but how to earn money?' her mum piped up.

'It's definitely doable, Mama. In fact, one of the brands that approached me offered 300 Ringgit for just one post about their products. I'm what they call a "micro-influencer".'

Mr Chong laughed and replied, '300 Ringgit? Can't even cover your *makan* (meals) for one week. You'll just starve.'

Mei could feel the anger rising within her, but she knew that an outburst of rage would do her no good. Through gritted teeth, she answered, 'Like I said, that's just one of the brands that contacted me. Plus, sponsorships are just one way of making money. Down the line, I can offer styling services and even launch my own line of products. This is just the beginning.'

Mei's mum raised her voice and reprimanded, 'Mei, what for you want to do all this when we already have a profitable family business? You know how hard your father work to provide for you and your sister? We are relying on you to carry on the family business. We are also getting old, you know. Cannot keep on working and supporting both of you forever. Don't be so selfish!'

However hard Mei tried to keep her cool, her mum somehow had the magical ability to push all her buttons.

'I'm grateful for all that you have done for me, but that doesn't mean I have to take over the family business when I so clearly don't want to. My passion is fashion and that's the business I want to pursue. I want to create something of my own, from the ground up, not inherit a business I haven't the slightest interest in.'

'So, what will happen to Chong & Co.?' Mr Chong asked as he flung Mei's phone across the table back to her.

'I don't know. Sue can run it if she wants to. Otherwise, sell the business and use the money to retire. Go travel the world.'

'How can you say that? This is our legacy . . . You want us to sell it just like that?' her mum asked melodramatically.

'No, I'm not telling you to sell it. Run the business yourselves, outsource it to someone else, do whatever you want. Just don't force me to take over when I keep telling you I don't want to.'

Mr Chong snickered, 'You think this Instant Gram thing—'

'Instagram,' Mei corrected.

'Whatever. You think this will bring you money? Put food on the table?'

'Yes. I'm confident that I'll be earning five figures in the next five years. This isn't just a pipe dream,' Mei replied confidently, eyeing her mum. 'It's a well-thought-out business plan. I'm sorry, but I'm not taking over Chong & Co.'

'Enough!' thundered Mr Chong as he shot out of his seat, his fists resting ominously on the dining table. 'I thought I raised you better than this. You disappoint me.' He stormed off, his food left untouched.

'See what you did? Your poor father never even eat anything,' Mei's mum snapped before going after him.

Mei sat alone at the table for a long time, as still as a statue, contemplating what to do next. Finally, she reached for her phone and deactivated her Instagram account. She buried her face in her arms on the table and wept, mourning the loss of her most precious possession.

Chapter 13

After a month, Maya was on her way back to Maestro. She had spent most of her semester break reading, indulging in her favourite Penang street food, and hanging out with Rohan and Mei virtually. Her mum was pretty busy with work, so it was mostly just Maya and her dad at home.

She had been given a few lectures by her dad about English literature being a waste of time and that she should switch to something more 'professional' and secure. Obviously, Maya's dad wasn't too thrilled about her wanting to be a writer. It used to bother her a lot, but now she felt quite indifferent about it. She had this one life to live, and she felt she owed it to herself to do what she loved. She could only hope that, in time, her father would come around to understand her.

As soon as her flight landed at Subang Airport, she got into a cab and headed to Maestro. Classes were scheduled to start the

following week, but Maya and Mei had a surprise in store for
Rohan, so they had both returned early. Rohan, who had stayed
on campus over the semester break, had kept himself occupied
by tutoring students online and exploring the city.

He hadn't wanted to waste a lot of money, so he visited all
the free attractions he could find. His favourites included Perdana
Botanical Garden, where he enjoyed solo picnics by the lake, and
Suria KLCC, where he camped for hours in their Kinokuniya
outlet reading graphic novels. He also researched all the must-try
cheap eats in KL and enjoyed trying the local delicacies like kueh,
cendol, nasi kandar, curry mee, and chicken rice.

When the cab pulled up in front of Maestro, Maya practically
jumped out and ran towards the cafeteria. Mei was already
waiting for her as planned. They hugged each other excitedly.

'I missed you,' Mei said.

'Me, too. I know we had video calls and all, but it just feels
so good to see you in person,' replied Maya.

They hurried to their dorm unit, chucked their bags in their
rooms, and headed down to Rohan's unit. Maya rang the bell and
shortly after, Rohan opened the door. The look of astonishment
on his face was priceless.

'What are you guys doing here?'

'Hello to you too!' Mei replied.

'Happy birthday, Rohan!' Maya gave him a warm embrace.

'Group hug,' Mei announced as she joined in.

'I thought you guys were coming back on Saturday.'

'Well . . . we decided to come back early to surprise you. No
way in hell were we going to let you spend your birthday alone.'

Rohan smiled, getting a little teary-eyed. Leaving home
was hard, but meeting Maya and Mei had made things so much
better. They were like family to him.

'All right, go get dressed. We're taking you out for dinner,'
Maya said, shooing Rohan back into his room.

'Wear something nice. Maya's found a cool place that you're going to love.'

* * *

'Didn't I tell you to wear something nice?' Mei said in exasperation.

'These are my best pair of jeans and my cleanest pair of sneakers,' defended Rohan.

Maya laughed. For the rest of their Grab ride, Rohan and Mei hotly debated men's fashion, specifically what was hot and what was not. Mei was of the opinion that jeans and sneakers were super casual, whereas Rohan vehemently argued that the look was versatile. Maya leaned her head against the window and looked out at the bright city lights.

After over an hour, thanks to peak hour traffic, they finally arrived at the restaurant that was located in one of the fancier parts of town. Mei swatted Rohan's hand away as he tried to pay for the ride and handed the driver 30 Ringgit. As they got out of the cab, Rohan saw that the signboard overhead read 'Flavours of India'. He smiled to himself. Leave it to his friends to know exactly what he was craving. They walked up the stairs to the entrance and a smiley waiter held the door open for them.

'Do you have a reservation, ma'am?' he asked.

'Yes. Maya Joseph, table for three,' Maya replied.

'Right this way, ma'am.'

The restaurant was packed. Maya had read online that the tables filled up pretty quickly, so she had made a reservation beforehand, just in case. The waiter showed them to their table towards the back of the long restaurant. They passed rows of tables surrounded by happy patrons and laden with mouth-watering dishes. Each table was lit with tealights and had small copper bowls with flowers floating on water, enhancing the ambience of the restaurant. Photographs of people and places in India covered the walls.

Once they sat down, their waiter served them warm water in copper tumblers. Soft Indian instrumental music played in the background as they studied the menu, aided by the warm lighting overhead. Maya noticed that Rohan was beginning to look a little uncomfortable.

She placed a reassuring hand on his shoulder and said, 'Rohan, tonight is our treat. Don't worry about the tab.'

'Guys, I can't let you pay for me. Everything here is so expensive!'

'And we absolutely can't let you pay on your birthday,' Mei rebutted.

'Rohan, it's our treat. And guess what, this place has your favourite: golgappas.'

'Really?' Rohan asked excitedly.

'Yes! So quit being a pain, and order something. I'm starving,' Mei replied.

'You choose. We're okay with anything,' Maya said, closing the menu and smiling at Rohan.

'Guys, I don't know what to say . . .' Rohan was touched. He was bummed about spending his birthday in KL, so far away from home, but Maya and Mei had surprised him by bringing a slice of home to him.

'Aiyyo, Rohan, no need to say anything, lah. Please, just order. People damn hungry here, okay?' Mei complained.

Rohan and Maya exchanged a meaningful glance. Mei's hangry streak had begun. They had to get some food in her. And fast.

'Excuse me,' Rohan called out to a passing waiter.

After fifteen minutes, their food arrived. Rohan's eyes lit up when he saw the golgappas. The deep-fried, hollow balls of dough, called puris, filled with spiced potatoes, were served with tamarind chutney and spicy mint-flavoured water on the side. Maya and Mei copied Rohan as he took a crispy puri in his hand, added some chutney to it, and dipped it in the mint water before popping the whole thing into his mouth.

Rohan, who obviously had tonnes of practice, made it look easy. Maya and Mei, on the other hand, struggled to eat the golgappas in one mouthful. Once Maya started to get the hang of it, she began to understand why Rohan loved this stuff. The tangy chutney and spicy mint water coupled with the crunch of the puris made for the perfect bite.

'Guys, these are so good,' Rohan said before popping another golgappa into his mouth.

'Excuse me, could we get another plate of golgappas, please?' Maya ordered.

Soon, their table was laden with more golgappas, soft chapatis, butter chicken, and palak paneer. They washed it all down with cool, refreshing mango lassi. For dessert, they ordered kulfi, a creamy Indian ice cream with cardamom and pistachios, and gulab jamun, deep-fried balls of sweetened dough served in sugar syrup. On the car ride back to Maestro, they felt full and satisfied, especially Rohan.

'Guys, for a moment there, I was seriously transported back to Delhi. I love exploring Malaysian food, but I'd been missing the food from home lately and tonight was just what I needed.'

'Bro, I'm happy that you're happy, but I really can't talk right now. Having a food coma over here,' Mei replied, looking really uncomfortable in her satin, baby pink bodycon dress.

Rohan saw an opportunity to make a point and took it. He loosened his belt and leaned back, linking his hands behind his head. 'See? This is why you should wear jeans,' he said with a cocky smile.

Mei gave Rohan a death stare and Maya tried hard not to laugh.

Chapter 14

A week later, the new semester kicked off. Maya, Rohan, and Mei had different classes and schedules, but they did sign up for one class together: macroeconomics. It was a compulsory subject for Rohan and Mei, both of whom wanted to minor in economics. For their majors, Rohan was set on doing finance and Mei was leaning towards marketing. Maya needed to complete three more electives, so she decided to go for another econs subject with her friends. Plus, Mr Ranjith would be teaching the subject and they loved him.

After their first macroeconomics lecture on a Wednesday afternoon, they decided to get lunch at the dorm café. As they enjoyed the day's special menu item, nasi lemak with sambal prawns, Maya got an email notification on her phone. She checked her email while Rohan and Mei debated which one of them would survive a zombie apocalypse.

'Oh my God!' Maya exclaimed. Rohan and Mei stopped arguing and turned towards her.

'What happened?' Mei asked.

'I got shortlisted for the National Short Story writing competition! Out of 350 submissions, 15 have been shortlisted for further review. And my story is one of them,' said Maya, barely able to contain her excitement.

'Dude, that's amazing! Congratulations,' replied Rohan.

'This calls for a celebration. Caramel frappés, on me,' said Mei before making a dash to the front counter to put in the order.

'Now, will you let me read your story?' asked Rohan.

Maya blushed and replied, 'Sure.'

She opened a PDF document on her phone and handed it over to Rohan. As Rohan started reading Maya's story, she said, 'Rohan, I hope you know . . . it's not that I don't want you to read my stories. I'm just not very confident as a writer—'

'Shh! I'm trying to concentrate,' Rohan said without shifting his gaze from Maya's phone.

Maya smiled and looked around at the other students in the café. She may have been shortlisted for the competition, but Maya still felt acutely self-conscious about Rohan reading her story. It felt almost as if she was baring her soul to the world. Rohan reached the end of Maya's story and smiled.

'Dude, it's really good.'

'Thanks, Rohan.'

'The main character, Devi . . . she's you, isn't she?'

'Sort of. I did get teased for my curly hair and dark skin when I was younger, but I wasn't as brave as Devi, though. I was too scared to stand up for myself back then.'

'You're braver than you think. You stood up to Susan Tan, didn't you?'

'I guess.'

'This story is pretty solid, Maya. You're for sure going to win this thing.'

Maya let out a nervous laugh. 'I don't know about that . . .'

Just then, Mei returned with a tray. 'As promised, three caramel frappés. Sorry for the delay, there was a long queue. Seems like everyone wants frappés today.'

'Cheers!' they clinked their mason jars before devouring the delicious frappés. Once they had emptied their jars, they strolled to the pool to enjoy the gentle evening breeze and sat down on a poolside bench in a comfortable silence. Rohan hummed a Hindi tune, while Maya clicked photos of the pool with the evening sky as a backdrop. Mei gazed quietly into the distance.

'Mei, hold that pose,' Maya said before snapping a picture of Mei. 'Babe, the lighting is perfect! And your pose is so natural. That's a new top, right? I don't think I've seen those earrings before either. Wait, let me post this pic on Insta and tag you.'

'No need, lah. Let's just put our phones aside and live in the moment.'

'Really? The forever-camera-ready fashionista is telling us to live in the moment?' Rohan teased.

Maya rolled her eyes and proceeded to upload the picture she took. 'Mei, why can't I tag you?' Maya looked at Mei with a perplexed expression.

Mei looked away, avoiding eye contact before shrugging casually, 'Oh, really? Must be some server error or something. I'm sure it'll sort itself out.'

'Wait, let me try,' Rohan chimed in before opening the app on his phone. 'Mei, I can't find your account. I can see Maya's profile and pics, but not yours . . . I don't think this is a server issue.'

Mei could feel her friends' eyes boring into her as they waited for an explanation. With a sigh of resignation, she turned to face them and said, 'Fine. You guys want the truth? I deactivated my account, okay?'

'WHAT? Why on earth would you do that?' Maya asked, appalled.

'I don't want to get my hopes up. My parents are never going to understand me or support my dream. I might as well give up now and just . . . do what they want me to do.'

'But your account was doing so well . . . you can't give up now.'

'D'you think I want to do this? D'you think it's not killing me inside?' Mei retorted, defensively. 'I have no choice, guys. If I don't do this, I'll just be a huge disappointment to my parents, and they'll hate me forever.' Her face crumpled as tears began flowing down her flushed cheeks. 'I really thought I could make them understand. I was a fool to even think that I could escape Chong & Co.'

'Babe, if we needed our parents' approval for everything, I wouldn't even be here right now,' Maya replied.

'But your mum supports you, Maya. Both my mama and papa don't support me. To them, fashion is just a huge waste of time.'

'Mei . . . it sucks to disappoint our parents, but we can't live our entire lives seeking their validation. I told you guys my parents wanted me to study business, right? Well, they wanted me to do my degree in India so I could be closer to home. But I really wanted to study abroad and explore the world a little. So, I applied for a scholarship here. They weren't happy about my decision, but I can't keep making them happy at my expense, you know? Sometimes you just have to put yourself first.'

Rohan went over to Mei and knelt down before her. She was taken aback, her tearful eyes widening in shock. He looked her in the eye and said, 'You get to put yourself first too,

Mei. You owe it yourself to at least try; see where this goes. It might fizzle out and go nowhere—'

'Great pep talk,' Mei mumbled.

'But it might also change your life. You have two years to build your brand, create something of your own like you've always wanted. If you make it, you'll have concrete evidence to prove to your parents that fashion isn't a waste of time. If you don't see a path forward . . .'

'. . . carve your own path to glory,' Maya ended.

Mei rolled her eyes and laughed through her tears. 'Only you dorks would remember the university motto and try to casually slip it into a conversation.'

'Well, it is the Maestro way,' Maya said, winking at Mei.

'So, what's it going to be, kid? Are you in or are you out?' Rohan asked, praying that his pep talk had worked.

In answer to his question, Mei took out her phone and reactivated her account. 'Happy?'

Maya squealed and hugged Mei tightly. She then proceeded to send the picture she had taken to Mei, who posted it on her account with the hashtag #carveyourownpathtoglory.

Chapter 15

The first two weeks of the semester were quite relaxing. The mad rush of assignments and tests usually kicked in from week three onwards. Maya, Rohan, and Mei braced themselves for a busy semester ahead. They were in their macroeconomics tutorial class with Mr Ranjith when they got their first assignment.

Good news: It was a thousand-word write-up about the macroeconomic policies adopted in recent years by any country of their choice. No more dreadful presentations.

Bad news: The assignment was to be done in pairs.

Shit. One of us will be left out, Rohan thought to himself. Mr Ranjith gave the class some time to form pairs. The class immediately burst into excited chatter.

'Er . . . what do we do, guys?' asked Rohan.

Just then, a tall, well-built boy walked over to Maya. 'Hey, I'm Dustin Lim,' he introduced himself and extended a hand.

Maya shook his hand and replied, 'Hi, I'm Maya.'

'Nice name,' said Dustin, flashing Maya a charming smile.

Wow! This guy's got a really nice set of teeth. And they're so white. He looks like he walked right out of a toothpaste commercial, Rohan thought to himself, starting to feel self-conscious about his own coffee-stained teeth.

'Thanks,' said Maya awkwardly.

'Do you wanna maybe do this assignment together?' Dustin asked.

Maya looked over at Rohan and Mei. This would solve their awkward predicament. 'Er . . . yeah, sure.'

'Great! I just met you, but here's my number. Call me, maybe?' Dustin grinned cheekily, referencing a popular song that Rohan hated with every fibre of his being. Dustin slipped Maya a piece of paper with his name and number on it. He flashed her another million-dollar smile and walked back to his seat at the back of the classroom.

'What a flirt! Sorry you got stuck with him,' said Rohan.

'Stuck with him? Are you blind? He's freakin' cute! I'm so jealous,' exclaimed Mei.

'I guess he's cute . . . if you subscribe to a mainstream idea of beauty and looks,' Rohan muttered.

Ignoring him, Maya turned around discreetly to take another look at Dustin. He had short, black hair, gelled and parted on the side. Maya was pretty sure Dustin worked out regularly given his toned physique, which he showed off in a well-fitting, black T-shirt and slim fit jeans. He paired that with white sneakers and a classic leather strap watch. Just then, Dustin caught Maya looking at him and flashed her another one of his killer smiles. Maya turned away anxiously, her heart beating a little faster than before.

'Mei, you're right. He is cute,' Maya whispered to her friends excitedly.

As Mr Ranjith resumed the lesson, Rohan found himself feeling hot around the ears and distracted.

After class, the three of them headed down to the café to have lunch when someone called out, 'Maya!'

She turned around to see Jonathan Liew, her classmate from creative writing 101 last semester, jogging towards her. He was Susan's favourite, but Maya tried hard not to hold it against him. He was a nice guy. Whenever she had asked to read his work, he was always obliging and never in a condescending way. And Maya had to admit, his work was good.

'Hey,' he said as he approached her.

'Hey, Jonathan. Long time no see. How are you?' Maya replied.

'I'm good. Actually, I wanted to congratulate you.'

'Congratulate me? For what?'

'I heard you were shortlisted for this year's national writing competition. That's huge. No one takes Maestro's English literature faculty seriously, so thank you for finally putting us on the map. Actually, I submitted a story as well, but it didn't make the cut,' he said, his cheeks turning a little red.

Maya smiled awkwardly, not quite knowing how to respond. She couldn't believe that the best writer in class was thanking her for putting Maestro on the map. Mei nudged her discreetly after a moment and Maya finally said, 'Thanks, Jonathan. I'm sure your story is awesome. I'd love to read it sometime.'

'No, lah, it's just a simple story—'

'I've read your stories before. Ms Susan always went on and on about them, so don't be so humble, okay?' Maya teased.

Jonathan's already red cheeks turned crimson. 'Okay, lah, you can read my story, but only if I can read yours.'

'Deal. I'll email it to you later.'

'Okay, catch you later, Maya,' Jonathan said before waving goodbye and walking off to class. Maya turned around to find her two friends beaming at her.

'Is that *the* Jonathan Liew?' Mei asked.

'Yes,' Maya replied trying hard to contain her excitement.

'You mean Susan Tan's can-do-no-wrong prodigy, Jonathan Liew?' Rohan further clarified.

'Uh-huh,' Maya nodded.

'And your story beat his? In a national level competition?' added Rohan cheekily.

Maya's hands flew to her cheeks, 'I can't believe it. They liked my story. Over Jonathan freakin' Liew's.'

'Hell yeah, they did!'

Maya couldn't contain her excitement any longer. She let out a shriek and jumped up, punching the air with her fists. As she did so, Dustin, who happened to be walking past them, couldn't help but smile at Maya's antics.

'Looking forward to working with you, partner,' he said before going down the stairs.

'Same here,' Maya replied, red in the face from embarrassment.

That was the day Maya finally got the proof she needed that she was a good writer. It was also the day Dustin, with his pearly whites, entered the picture. Rohan had mixed feelings about that day.

* * *

Maya's excitement died down over the weekend when the winner of the competition was announced. She hadn't made the cut. The rejection email sent to her was generic, offering little comfort:

Dear participant,

We are sorry to inform you that your story has not been selected as the winning entry this year.

It was a difficult task choosing between so many talented writers, but the judges finally decided to go with 'Of Rackets and Shuttlecocks' by Mohd Ridzuan Sabaruddin as this year's winner.

Thank you for your entry and we look forward to your participation next year.

Maya received this email on Saturday and spent all day moping in bed. She didn't tell her friends. They had been so excited for her and she didn't quite know how to break the bad news to them. She lied to them instead, telling them that she had to work on an English literature assignment that was due on Monday, just so she could grieve in the solitude of her dorm room. Avoiding Mei was particularly challenging since they stayed in the same dorm unit, but Maya insisted that she needed to be completely alone so she could focus on her killer writing assignment. Mei just rolled her eyes in response, mumbling something about how weird creatives can be. In any case, neither of them disturbed Maya and she spent the day eating junk food in bed.

On Sunday morning, nothing had changed. But she was somehow even more miserable than she had been the previous day. So much for time heals all wounds. As her thoughts spiralled, she began to seriously question her talent. If she wasn't a writer, what was she? While battling this identity crisis, her phone pinged. She reached for it, wondering what excuse to give her friends to bail on dinner, but it wasn't Rohan or Mei. It was an email from someone she didn't know.

Dear Maya,

By now, you already know that your story wasn't chosen as the winning entry for this year's short story competition.

If you're anything like me, you're probably moping around your room, questioning your life choices.

Well, I was once your age, and I know a thing or two about being a young writer who hasn't quite found her footing in the big, scary world of publishing and literature. So let me set your mind at ease.

I read your story and loved it. At such a young age, you've managed to find your voice as a writer and create characters who are relatable and compelling. You may not have won this year, but trust me, you came close.

Do me a favour. Keep writing. Whatever insecurities or doubts you may have, just keep writing. Take it from me, doubting yourself is part of the process. You have a gift. Hone it.

I look forward to reading more of your stories soon.

All the best.

Yours truly,
Kanmani Rajeshwaran,
Author, Two-Time Winner of the Asian Bookerman Award, and Lead Judge of the 2017 Malaysian National Short Story Writing Competition

Tears started flowing down Maya's face.
You have a gift. Hone it.
She read and re-read those words over and over again in disbelief. All this time, she had doubted herself and had questioned her worth as a writer. Finally, she had the validation she needed.
You have a gift. Hone it.
Words that would forever be etched in her heart and soul.
Keep writing. Whatever insecurities or doubts you may have, just keep writing.
In that moment, she promised herself that she would do just that.

Chapter 16

A few days later, Rohan and Mei were having coffee in the dorm café after class. As usual, they were engrossed in an intense debate. This time, it was about Mr Park, their corporate finance lecturer.

'I think he's a sadist. That's got to be it. How else do you explain the 60 per cent failing rate for his class? He's intentionally making the paper tough to see us suffer,' Mei scowled angrily.

'Look, I don't want to fail just as much as the next guy, but I don't think Mr Park is out to get us. The topic he covers is complex in nature, that's all,' Rohan defended him.

Mei rolled her eyes in response. 'I know you're his favourite and all—'

'I'm not,' Rohan denied, his cheeks turning red. 'He's got a bad rep as being a psycho, but he's actually quite a decent lecturer, Mei. It's not his fault that the subject matter is ridiculously challenging. He inherited the subject and syllabus from his predecessor, Prof. Matthews, you know? He's working on changing it next year.'

'And how do you know that?' Mei raised her eyebrow.

'Well . . . we were chatting during office hours and he told me,' Rohan shrugged casually, trying to avoid eye contact with Mei.

'Bro, no one just "casually chats" with a lecturer in their office. You're definitely his blue-eyed boy. Probably because you're the only one who bothers to attempt his impossible tutorial questions before class.'

'For the last time, I'm not the teacher's pet, okay? By the way, where's Maya?' Rohan asked, desperately trying to change the topic.

'She's meeting with Dustin to discuss the econs assignment.'

'Again? Didn't they already meet yesterday?'

'Partners are allowed to meet more than once for an assignment, you know. If I were Maya, I'd take any excuse to meet Dustin,' said Mei, smiling cheekily.

'Well, you're not Maya. I hope he's not taking advantage of her and getting her to do all the donkey work,' Rohan replied sullenly.

'Like what you did last semester?'

Rohan glared at Mei, 'I wasn't taking advantage; I was taking care of Cocoa! Plus, we did do the assignment together in the end.'

'If you say so,' Mei acquiesced.

Just then, Maya walked in and joined them. 'Hey,' she said as she set her backpack on the floor and sat down beside Rohan.

'So, how was your meeting with Pearly Whites?' asked Mei curiously.

'It was good. We've decided to go with Canada for our assignment,' Maya replied with a coy smile.

'Is that it? You've been meeting up with him for over two days and all you guys have done is choose the country?' Rohan asked in disbelief.

'Hey, that's good progress. Choosing the right country is crucial. We did some research and agreed that Canada would be an interesting country to write about,' Maya replied, defensively.

'When are you meeting him again?' Mei asked, ignoring Rohan's weird vibe. She couldn't believe Rohan was being so dense. Hopefully he'd pick up on what was going on soon enough.

'Tomorrow. We're gonna do more research over coffee.'

'That's so exciting. What are you going to wear?' Mei followed up.

Rohan snickered and replied, 'What does it matter? She's working on an econs assignment, not sashaying down a runway.'

Maya ignored Rohan's remark and said, 'I was thinking of wearing my flowy, floral dress with a cute pair of flats.'

'You mean the outfit you wore to Rohan's birthday dinner?' Mei asked to clarify. Maya nodded excitedly and Mei replied, 'Good choice. That dress looks gorgeous on you. Why not go with wedges? I'll lend you a pair.'

'Ooh, that sounds perfect.'

'Isn't that dress kind of fancy for a group discussion?' Rohan chimed in.

'You've got much to learn, my Padawan. It's not just a group discussion. It could become so much more,' Mei said, nudging Maya who had begun to blush rosily.

'Why does it feel like there's something you guys aren't telling me?' Rohan asked suspiciously.

'Well . . . I think he's kind of cute,' Maya said.

'So?' he replied, not getting the point.

Maya looked over at Mei for some help. 'Rohan, what do you do when you meet a cute girl?' asked Mei. Seeing the puzzled expression on Rohan's face, she added, 'You try to talk to her, get to know her. See if it could develop into something more, right? That's what's happening here. Geez. I know your parents are strict and all, but have you never pursued a girl before?'

'Look, I'm not a prude. I've had crushes before, and I've done all kinds of things to get their attention; but that was back in high school. I'd like to think I've matured since then.'

'What's that supposed to mean? Are you implying that I'm somehow immature?' Maya demanded, anger instantly swelling up inside her.

'No, that's not what I'm saying. I mean, what do we even know about this guy? Other than the fact that he has poor taste in music. Isn't it a little superficial to focus on looks—'

'Oh, now I'm both immature *and* superficial?' Maya replied, her tone dripping with sarcasm.

Rohan sighed, 'Maya, all I'm saying is, get to know the guy first. Don't start throwing yourself at him without knowing the first thing about him.'

'Throwing myself at him? Are you kidding me right now? I'm not throwing myself at him, Rohan. I'm putting myself out there. There's a big difference. All I'm doing is picking out something to wear for when I meet a cute guy I kind of have a crush on. And you're twisting this innocent thing into something horrible,' Maya's voice rose in anger.

Students seated at the other tables began to look over at them.

'Maya, I'm just looking out for you.'

'I don't need you looking out for me. Mind your own damn business,' she snapped and stormed out of the café.

'Not cool, bro,' said Mei, before hurrying after Maya.

Rohan was left alone at the table and all eyes were on him. *What the hell just happened?* he wondered.

* * *

'Thanks, Mei. I'll return these soon,' Maya said as she slipped on Mei's wedges.

'You look amazing. The shoes really tie your outfit together. Have fun with Dustin,' Mei replied, winking at Maya playfully.

'Thanks, babe. See you later.'

Maya left her dorm unit and headed downstairs. She was in her floral dress and cute wedges with her hair drawn back in a ponytail, which drew focus to Maya's long neck and gold hoop earrings. *Screw, Rohan. I'm allowed to wear whatever I want. I don't need his permission. Who does he think he is, anyway?* Maya brooded angrily. She made her way to the front gate where Dustin was waiting for her in his car. She got in and Dustin drove off.

'Hey, Dustin. Thanks for picking me up,' said Maya.

'No problem. I was getting sick of the mediocre coffee they serve on campus. I've been craving a really good cup of cappuccino. I know a place nearby that makes great coffee. You like coffee too, right?'

'Guilty. I'm a huge caffeine-addict.'

'Great! We'll order some coffee and get to work.'

After about ten minutes, they arrived at The Sunrise Café. Dustin parked his car, and they made their way inside. It was a cozy café that gave Maya Starbucks vibes. Upbeat music played in the background as they ordered their drinks at the counter. The display case featured a variety of different cakes including cheesecake, red velvet, black forest, rainbow, and others. The menu overhead was pretty standard for a coffee shop and included all the usual suspects: americanos, lattes, cappuccinos, teas, and frappés.

Maya ordered a mocha frappé and Dustin got himself a cappuccino. Then, they walked over to a table in the corner and sat down. They connected to the free Wi-Fi and got to work. They read up on the macroeconomic policies implemented in Canada and came up with an outline for their write-up. As they continued to do more research, Maya couldn't help but peek at Dustin over her laptop. He wore a close-fitting, grey T-shirt that showed off his toned arms and body. With one hand on his chin and one raised eyebrow, Maya could tell that he was concentrating hard on the task at hand, just as she should have been doing, but she was too distracted to make sense of the fiscal and monetary policies displayed on her screen. Just then, almost as if he sensed Maya's scrutiny, Dustin looked up and their eyes locked. Maya's heart started racing. Dustin flashed her his signature smile and Maya smiled awkwardly in return, before hastily shifting her focus to her screen.

Three hours and many more stolen glances later, they had divided the remaining work between the two of them and decided to call it a day.

'That was a very productive session. I think we've earned a treat. Cheesecake? It's on me,' Dustin offered.

'Sure.'

Dustin went over to the front counter and got them each a slice of cheesecake. 'Here you go, milady,' said Dustin, as he put the plates down on the table.

'Thank you. Honestly, I had my eye on the cheesecake ever since we got here.'

Dustin laughed and said, 'Great minds think alike, I guess.'

They started chatting and Maya got to know Dustin a little better. He was a business student like Mei and Rohan, hoping to major in marketing and business law. His goal was to launch a start-up of his own and become a millionaire by the time he hit thirty.

'Why thirty? Isn't that a lot of pressure to put on yourself?' Maya asked curiously.

'I guess it is a lot of pressure, but I'm the sort of person who thrives under pressure. In fact, I usually do all my assignments last minute. The night before they're due, to be exact. That's when the adrenaline kicks in and I do my best work,' Dustin replied.

'Really? But we started working on this assignment pretty early on.'

Dustin smiled and said, 'Yeah, I was pretty eager to get started on this one. Probably because I'm paired with the prettiest girl in class.'

Maya blushed, 'Oh . . . thanks. But I don't think I'm the prettiest girl in class. Mei's way prettier than I am.'

'There are a lot of pretty girls in class, but I stand by what I said.' Dustin flashed his pearly whites at Maya and her heart skipped a beat.

Maya tried to casually brush aside the fact that Dustin was obviously flirting with her and said, 'Thanks for breaking your rule about working on assignments last minute for me. I hate working in high-pressure situations. My friends and I worked on a presentation pretty last minute once and I couldn't stand it!'

'You're welcome. I'm really enjoying our work sessions.'

'Me too. Oh, I don't think I mentioned earlier, I'm an English literature major.'

'Really? I thought you were majoring in business. Why English literature? There isn't much money in that, right?'

Maya winced a little at Dustin's words. Generalized statements about English literature being a poor man's choice were a real trigger for Maya after all the family drama with her dad.

'Well, there's more to life than just money, you know. I love literature and I hope to be a writer one day.'

'Sure, there's more to life than just money; but you do need money for a lot of things. Like your mocha frappés and this cheesecake.' Dustin gestured towards the table with a smug look on his face.

'Dustin, I didn't ask you to buy me this cheesecake. And I'd rather forgo some luxuries than work a job I have no interest in.'

'Are we having our first fight?' Dustin asked with a naughty glint in his eyes.

His flirting, which Maya initially found flattering, was now annoying her. 'This isn't a fight. I'm just pointing out that people are different, Dustin. I respect that you want to be a millionaire before you turn thirty and I think you should respect that I want to be a writer.'

'I'm sorry, I didn't mean to offend you . . . but you know the odds of becoming a famous writer is like one in a million, right? For every Stephen King, there are hundreds of wannabe writers who didn't make it. It's a risky business, that's all.' Seeing the sullen expression on Maya's face, he quickly added, 'Not that you're a wannabe or anything. I'm sure you're very talented. Maybe I can read your writing sometime?' He flashed her his blinding smile and added a wink for good measure.

'Yeah, maybe,' Maya replied, desperately wanting this work-session-cum-chat to be over. She looked down at her watch and said, 'It's getting late. I think I'd better head back.'

'I'll give you a ride back to campus,' Dustin replied.

'No, it's fine. I think I'll book a Grab. It's out of the way for you anyway.'

'Are you sure? It's really no problem.'

'Yeah, I'm sure.' An awkward silence ensued as Maya tried hard to control her anger. She opened her Grab app and managed to book a ride. Thankfully, it was just two minutes away. Maya opened her purse, fished out some cash and handed it over to Dustin. 'And here's my half for the cheesecake.'

'Hey, no. It's my treat. You don't have to pay me.'

'No, I prefer to go Dutch, fifty-fifty,' she insisted, her hand still held out. Dustin awkwardly took the cash and pocketed it. 'Thanks for the ride earlier, Dustin. I'll finish up my part for the assignment this week.'

'Sure. Maybe we can meet up next week to compile the assignment together? I know another great café not too far—' Dustin started, before Maya cut him off.

'I'm pretty busy next week. I don't mind compiling the assignment on my own. Just e-mail me your part once you're done.'

'Oh . . . okay.'

'Bye, Dustin,' Maya said before walking out of the café and getting into the Grab car. *Shit! Was Rohan right?*

* * *

A week later, Maya was still furious at Dustin. He had just sent over his part of the assignment, and she was putting it all together. Just as she was finishing up, her phone pinged: *Hey . . . you okay?*

Maya rolled her eyes. It was the fifth text from Dustin that week. *Can't he take a hint?* she thought to herself. Ping.

Haven't heard from you in a while . . . did you get my email?

'So that's why he keeps texting me. Just to see if I'm done with the assignment. What a selfish prick. Have the decency to apologize first, you dickhead,' Maya almost screamed out loud.

She was so done with this assignment. As soon as she filled in the details on the cover page, she uploaded the assignment online and took a screenshot of the submission page. She then forwarded the pic to Dustin with the colder-than-ice caption, 'Done.'

He reacted to her message with a thumbs up, which only riled Maya even more.

Before really thinking things through, she opened her Instagram app and posted the screenshot she took on her stories. She typed out—*Finally done with this group assignment from hell. Just my luck to get stuck with the worst partner! #storyofmylife*, and hit share.

The small voice of reason in the back of Maya's mind spoke up just about then. *Dustin follows you on Instagram. He's going to see it.*

She told that voice to shut up and did what she usually did when faced with difficult feelings: curled up in bed and pulled the covers over her head. It didn't make her feelings disappear, but she did manage to squeeze in a good nap though.

Maya was awoken a few hours later by the incessant pinging of her phone. Groggily, she reached out for it and checked the notifications. It was a series of messages from Dustin. She shot out of bed in panic.

Are you serious???

I did my part and sent it to you in time!

You're the one who ignored all my messages.

I say one wrong thing and this is how you react?? Real mature Maya! Grow up and learn to deal with your emotions like an adult!

Maya's hands shook as she read Dustin's unfiltered messages, beads of sweat trailing down her face.

'Shit, shit, SHIT!' she spiralled as she slipped back under the covers, hoping the darkness would swallow her whole.

Chapter 17

Maya walked into her econs tutorial class the next day and sat down beside Mei. Rohan, who sat on the other side of Mei, looked over at Maya, but she was still giving him the cold shoulder. Things may have taken a weird turn with Dustin, but what Rohan had said wasn't right. Maya was still mad at him. Also, she didn't want to give him the satisfaction of knowing about her disastrous coffee date.

'Hey, have you submitted the assignment?' Mei asked.

'Yep, sent it in last night.'

'Same here.' Mei leaned in closer to Maya and whispered, 'I saw your Insta story yesterday, before you deleted it. So . . . things aren't going well with Dustin?'

'You saw that?' Maya winced in embarrassment. She was hoping the world had somehow overlooked her lapse of judgement.

'Yeah . . . what was that about?'

'I don't know . . . I was hoping to talk to him today, but he isn't here. I hope he didn't skip class because of me.'

'Nah, maybe something came up. You'll catch him next time.'

After the tutorial class, Mei and Rohan had a replacement accounting lecture to attend, so Maya headed to the campus cafeteria for a solo lunch. She ordered a plate of spicy fried rice with extra prawns. The *mak cik* (aunty) who ran the goreng-goreng stall, which sold a variety of fried rice and noodle dishes, was an experienced and efficient cook. She cooked in a sturdy wok over a large flame, adding ingredients and tossing them skilfully. Maya often ordered food from her stall just to watch her work her magic.

Within five minutes, the mak cik had prepared a steaming hot plate of fried rice for Maya with a generous helping of prawns and fish cake. The mak cik also knew that Maya liked her food spicy, so she added chopped bird's eye chilli in soy sauce on the side for her. Maya didn't realize just how hungry she was until the fragrant smell of the fried rice wafted up towards her. She started salivating and couldn't wait to dig in. After thanking the mak cik, she made her way to their usual spot under the tree. The weather was sunny, but not overly hot. Maya enjoyed the gentle breeze as she settled down at the table. Before coming to Maestro, she had always hated the idea of dining alone. For the first few weeks, she would always order takeaway and eat in her room whenever she was flying solo.

However, the campus environment started to grow on Maya. She enjoyed sitting in the cafeteria, immersed in the energy and excitement that the campus often buzzed with. There was always something or other going on near the cafeteria. As Maya started eating, she noticed a group of boys in the corner doing flips and cheering each other on loudly as one of them filmed their stunts. The table next to Maya was occupied by a group of friends playing some board game she had never seen before. The board was filled with tokens, some that took the shape of characters like elves and wizards, and others that resembled structures such as houses and taverns. She guessed it must be some game like Dungeons and Dragons, set in medieval times.

Although the fried rice had been skilfully made, Maya wasn't enjoying it as much as she usually did. She kept thinking about Dustin and the messages he had sent her. How could she have been so stupid? Deep down, she knew that venting on social media was never helpful, but she had been angry and hadn't been thinking straight. If only she could talk to Dustin . . .

Just as Maya was about to give up on her fried rice, she serendipitously saw Dustin in the distance. She cleared her plate and hastily made her way towards him. He was walking with earphones on, so he didn't hear her approach. When she was just a few steps away, Dustin thought he heard something and spun around. Maya couldn't stop in time and ended up colliding into Dustin. They fell to the ground and the books which Dustin was carrying in his arms flew into the air. Maya shielded her face as they came tumbling down on them.

'What the hell is your problem?' Dustin yelled as he got up and started gathering his books.

'I'm sorry. That was an accident,' Maya exclaimed as she helped him pick up the books.

'What do you want, Maya?' Dustin spat out angrily as he forcefully shoved the books into his backpack.

'I texted you last night—'

'Well, seeing that you didn't bother to reply any of my messages this whole week, I figured I'd return the favour,'

Dustin shot Maya a cold look as he swung his backpack, which was bursting at the seams, over his shoulder.

Maya winced at the barb. 'Yeah . . . I guess I deserve that. Look, can we talk?'

Dustin considered this question for a moment before replying, 'Fine.'

They found a vacant table and Maya offered to buy them drinks, which Dustin refused.

'Dustin . . . I shouldn't have posted that story yesterday. I was upset with you, yeah, but you didn't deserve that. You did your part well and you were a pretty good partner.'

'Yeah, it was really sucky of you to post that, Maya. Half of our class follows you on Instagram. Everyone knows who you're referring to.'

'Is that why you didn't come to class today?' Maya asked, flooded with remorse.

Dustin nodded. Maya covered her face with her hands. 'Oh, my God, I'm so sorry, Dustin. I really wasn't thinking straight.'

'Well, I did have to collect these textbooks from a senior . . . so it wasn't all you,' Dustin replied. 'Maya, why didn't you reply to any of my texts?'

'To be honest . . . I was angry with you.'

'Yeah, no shit! Why were you so angry?'

'I hate it when people say writing isn't a smart choice . . . I get enough of that at home,' Maya replied, crossing her arms defensively. 'We were getting on so well and then you had to go and say those things . . . it just completely changed the vibe, you know?'

Dustin nodded slowly as he considered Maya's words.

'Okay . . . I see what you're saying. I'm sorry, Maya, I didn't mean to offend you,' Dustin said slowly. He leaned forward with his arms on the table, looking intently at Maya. 'In my family, money is a big deal. We were always told that we must study hard and get high-paying jobs or else cannot get any *lengloi* . . . pretty girls,' Dustin added for good measure, in case Maya wasn't familiar with the Cantonese term. Maya couldn't help but smile and shake her head. That was such an Asian parent thing to say.

'I guess I was sort of projecting all of that on to you and that wasn't cool,' he shook his head regretfully. 'So, I get why you got triggered. But why didn't you just talk to me about it? Why did you ignore me and then choose to blast it out on social media instead?' Dustin asked, clearly hurt by the way Maya had chosen to deal with the situation.

'I'm sorry, Dustin. That was really immature of me. I should have just told you how I felt instead of being so passive-aggressive,' Maya replied, her cheeks burning with shame.

'I guess we all make mistakes . . . but I wish yours wasn't so public, lah,' Dustin said in frustration.

'I know this doesn't make up for what I did, but let's try something . . .' Maya then whipped out her phone and took a selfie with Dustin. She posted it on Instagram with the caption: *JK before. Lucky to be paired with the smartest guy in class! #mygroupmateisbetterthanyours*, and tagged Dustin.

He laughed and reshared the story.

'Look, the likes are coming in. And it's mostly our classmates,' Maya announced.

'Well, I guess your damage control plan worked.'

'Dustin . . . how about we put all this behind us and start again? Friends?' Maya extended her hand, hoping it wasn't too little, too late.

Dustin smiled and shook her hand. 'Friends. Now, how about that drink?'

* * *

As they were chatting over drinks, Dustin expressed his interest in rock climbing and Maya made the mistake of telling him that she had climbed the Maestro wall along with Esther the previous semester. Dustin got excited and insisted that Maya show him the ropes since he had never done it before. Maya tried to point out that she pretty much sucked at the sport, but Dustin was having none of it. He was of the opinion that some experience was better than no experience at all.

'You owe me,' he insisted.

'Arghhhh! Fine. But after this, we're even, okay?' And that is how Maya found herself face-to-face with the formidable wall once again. *We meet again, old foe,* she thought to herself.

Dustin had gone up before her and much like Esther, he seemed to have a natural aptitude for scaling walls. Maya couldn't believe it was his first time.

'Are you sure you haven't done this before? Or was that just a ruse to get me to join you?' asked Maya, cocking an eyebrow in suspicion.

'I swear it's my first time. Just beginner's luck, I guess,' Dustin replied flashing his signature pearly whites.

Maya cursed this elusive beginner's luck that seemed to strike everyone but her; she also made a mental note to introduce Dustin to Esther one day. Perhaps those two could scale walls together and leave her out of it. Although it was an arduously slow process, Maya eventually managed to make it to the top of the wall and slammed the buzzer (again).

Dustin cheered and even whistled to celebrate Maya's climb to the top. Chandran, the rock climbing operator who was witnessing Maya's shame for the second time, did not share Dustin's enthusiasm. He was supposed to go for his lunch break five minutes ago and was getting hangry.

'Okay, guys, your time is up. Return the gear and collect your deposit,' he said as he looked at his watch and walked away to his office.

Maya cautiously swung down and then took off her harness. 'I'm sure Chandran thinks I'm a loser,' she muttered, feeling very self-conscious.

'No, lah. I'm sure he thinks you're . . . fine,' Dustin said, hoping his white lie sounded convincing.

'Wow, you're a terrible liar,' Maya replied as she playfully punched his shoulder.

'I'm sorry, but it kinda looked like you were going in slow-mo,' Dustin pursed his lips tightly, trying hard to suppress a laugh.

Maya rolled her eyes. 'I told you I sucked at this. Now I've made a fool of myself—twice!'

'Well, I found it pretty entertaining,' Dustin replied smugly. Maya flipped him off in response. They returned their gear and joined Mei for lunch at the dorm café where, to Maya's horror, Dustin shared details of her embarrassing climb that left Mei in stitches.

A few weeks later, Maya was still not speaking to Rohan. She felt Rohan owed her an apology and the fact that, after all this time, he still hadn't approached her to apologize made Maya even angrier. After an econs tutorial one day, as Maya was packing up her things, Dustin came over and put a flyer on the table in front of her.

Rohan, two seats down, started packing at a snail's pace. He was curious about what was going on between Maya and Pearly Whites. Rohan had asked Mei about the two of them, only to get shot down. Mei refused to break Girl Code and dish on Maya's love life (as she put it), at least not until Rohan apologized. Maya looked down at the flyer that read:

The Foodie Club presents Cooking with the Stars!

Join this one-time-only cooking class,
led by celebrity chef Daniel Tan,
with a friend and learn from a PRO!
Limited slots available. Sign up now!

P.S. The duo with the best tasting dish will win a prize!
Bring your A-game, folks!

'You thinking of joining?' Maya asked in surprise.

'Yeah . . . I know it's lame—'

'No, it sounds fun,' Maya reassured. 'I didn't know you could cook.'

'It's a new hobby, actually.'

'That's awesome. How come the sudden interest in cooking?'

'Well . . . you're so passionate about writing and it kinda made me want to find my own thing too, you know? I've always been a foodie, so I thought I'd give it a shot,' Dustin replied, his cheeks turning a little red.

'Wahh, I inspired you, eh?' Maya teased.

'Yeah, yeah, don't let it go to your head.'

'Jokes aside, I'm sure you'll do great. I'll be rooting for you,' Maya replied with a smile as she continued to pack her things.

'Yeah . . . about that . . . they only allow people to sign up in pairs. I can't really join this thing on my own. So I was thinking . . .'

Maya froze. 'Are you asking me to team up with you?' Dustin nodded in response. 'But, bro, the only thing I can cook is Maggi. And that too in the microwave,' Maya replied, horrified.

'Please, Maya, no one else wants to join me. They don't want to waste a Saturday coming to campus for this thing.'

'So, I'm your last resort?' Maya asked with a raised eyebrow.

'Er . . . no, I just saved best for last.'

'Nice cover.'

'Look, don't worry, I'll do all the cooking. And if we win, you can have the prize. I just wanna join the competition and get a chance to talk to Chef Daniel. I follow his cooking channel on YouTube and his videos are amazing,' Dustin gushed.

Maya could relate to desperately wanting to meet someone you admire. Although it didn't turn out so well with her and Susan Tan, Chef Daniel could be different. Dustin could get inspired and learn a thing or two from him.

'Fine. I'll join with you,' she said with a sigh.

'Thank you, thank you, thank you! You're a lifesaver, Maya. I'll go sign us up,' Dustin replied excitedly before dashing out of the classroom.

As Maya finished packing up, she noticed Rohan looking over at her. 'What?' she asked rudely.

Rohan got flustered and blurted out, 'Er . . . nothing . . . just surprised you agreed to compete in a cooking competition.'

'Well, that's what friends do. But I wouldn't expect you to understand,' Maya said sharply before heaving her backpack over her shoulder and leaving the classroom.

Mei glared at Rohan.

'What? I didn't do anything,' he said defensively.

'Why don't you just apologize already?' Mei replied.

'I don't think it would make any difference, Mei. You heard what she said. She's still mad at me. The last thing she wants to do right now is talk to me.'

'Rohan, what you said to her about the whole Dustin thing wasn't cool. If you value your friendship with Maya and you want to make things right, I suggest you come down from your high horse and say sorry,' Mei said before she left the room, leaving Rohan behind to ponder on her words.

Chapter 18

Maya burst out of her room and raced downstairs to Maestro's outdoor foyer area. She could have sworn that she had set her alarm for 8 a.m. She must have switched it off in a sleepy haze and gone back to sleep.

Shit, shit, shit! I'm late. Dustin is gonna kill me, Maya thought to herself. As soon as the elevator doors opened, she zoomed out of the dorm building and into campus. She raced past the cafeteria at top speed until she reached the foyer.

The foyer was a beautiful outdoor space next to Maestro's open field. It had tall, majestic trees on one side and faced the business school building. The foyer, being a wide empty space, was frequently used for campus events. On that particular day, the foyer was set up with rows of tables. Each table had been equipped with a hot plate, chopping board, a knife, a wide array of ingredients, and a set of aprons. Maya spotted Dustin behind one of the tables and hurried over to him.

'Sorry I'm late,' Maya said breathlessly. 'I slept through my alarm.'

'Hey, I thought you ditched me.'

'Of course not, lah. So little faith you have in me!'

Dustin laughed jovially and winked at Maya. 'Anyway, don't worry, Chef Daniel isn't here yet. He's running late.'

'Thank God.'

For the next half hour, all the contestants waited restlessly for the cooking lesson to start. Some wandered off to the field to sit down and scroll through their phones. Others sat around the tables, chatting with their partners and snacking on the chopped vegetables. Dustin, who had bumped into an old school friend, was catching up with him.

'Hey, Maya, we're heading to the vending machine to get some coffee. D'you want to join us?' Dustin asked.

'Nah, I'm good. You guys go ahead,' Maya replied. She started scrolling through her phone when she heard a familiar voice.

'Hey.'

Maya looked up to see Rohan standing in front of her. He was in his usual outfit—faded blue jeans, a chequered shirt over a plain white tee, and sneakers.

'What are you doing here?' Maya asked.

'I thought I'd come and show my support,' Rohan replied coyly.

'Oh,' Maya said, not quite knowing what to say.

'Maya . . . I'm sorry. I shouldn't have said what I said. It was stupid and judgemental. You're a smart, capable person who can make her own decisions. And Dustin seems like a nice guy. I'm happy for you guys.'

'Happy for us?' Maya said, holding back her laughter. 'Rohan, we're not together. I know we haven't been speaking to each other for a few weeks now, but my love life is still the same as before—boring and uneventful. Dustin and I are just friends.'

'Oh. I'm sorry, I didn't mean to jump to conclusions,' Rohan said, worried that he may have said the wrong thing once again.

'No, that's okay. Rohan . . . why did it take you so long to come talk to me? Friends fight and that's normal, but I thought you'd come speak to me sooner. The past few weeks have been hell for me, you idiot.'

'They've been hell for me too. I kept wanting to come and talk to you, but I was scared. I wasn't sure if you'd ever want to speak to me again. I said some really stupid stuff and I was worried that I had crossed a line of no return. As long as I didn't speak to you, there was still a chance we could remain friends. But if I spoke to you and you didn't want to be friends any more, that would be . . . final, you know?' Rohan said, looking dolefully down at his shoes. He continued, 'I'm sorry, I know it was stupid. I should've apologized sooner.'

Maya hugged Rohan, which caught him by surprise. 'It's not stupid, you idiot. I get it. I don't want to lose you as a friend either. But there's nothing we can't talk through and sort out, okay?'

'Okay,' Rohan said as relief washed over his face.

Just then, Chef Daniel arrived and all the contestants hurried back to their tables. Dustin speedwalked back to Maya's side, a coffee in hand.

'Good luck, guys. Save some food for me,' said Rohan encouragingly before jogging over to the sidelines.

The next two hours flew by. Chef Daniel walked them through how to make Nyonya-style chicken curry and mixed vegetables. As Chef Daniel provided step-by-step instructions, the contestants followed his lead to replicate his recipe.

Maya had agreed to sign up for this thing only for Dustin's sake. She had no real experience or interest in cooking. Maya struggled with the very first step: peeling ginger. As promised, Dustin ended up doing most of the heavy lifting. He swiftly prepared the ingredients for the spice paste and pounded them in a mortar and pestle on the ground. He then proceeded to sauté the spice paste in oil. Most contestants were craning their necks or hurrying to the front to get a closer look at what Chef Daniel was doing, but Dustin merely listened carefully and followed his instructions diligently.

While the chicken curry was cooking, Dustin followed Chef Daniel's lead and started preparing ingredients such as cabbage, mustard leaves, carrots, and mushrooms for the mixed vegetables dish.

Meanwhile, Maya tried desperately to devein some fresh prawns but found the knifework challenging due to her overall lack of dexterity. Once Dustin prepped the vegetables, he came to her rescue and took over.

Maya moved on to the simpler task of soaking beancurd sheets. Soon after, Dustin started stir-frying the vegetables, demonstrating some impressive tossing skills in the process. For a moment there, Maya was reminded of the mak cik from the campus cafeteria. Maya was just staring at Dustin, completely in awe of his recently acquired skills, and had to remind herself to make it look like she was doing something remotely helpful. So, she stirred the chicken curry and waved her hands above the pot to guide the wafting aromas towards her nose. She smelled the curry, gave an approving nod, and continued to stir.

'Many of you are home cooks who are eager to learn. When we first start learning how to cook at home, we get very excited and we want to try everything, especially Western dishes like pasta and pizza. But here's my advice—don't forget our local delights. The best teachers are inside our own homes. Ask your parents or grandparents to teach you how to make their signature dishes. That is how I started learning how to cook,' Chef Daniel said as he put the finishing touches for his dishes. He then proceeded to walk around the foyer, inspecting everyone's technique and progress. Chef Daniel stopped at every table and offered tips and suggestions.

When he reached Maya's table, Dustin was chopping chillies for garnish. Chef Daniel asked to take over and demonstrated the correct knife technique to prevent personal injuries. He handed the reins back to Dustin, and before leaving for the next table, he said, 'The curry smells on point. Good job.'

'Thank you, Chef,' Dustin beamed from ear to ear.

After ten minutes or so, all the contestants had finished cooking and it was time for Chef Daniel to taste everyone's dishes and pick a winner for the day. As he moved from table to table, tasting every dish, he remained poker-faced, providing no indication as to which dishes he preferred. When he was done, he walked to the front of the foyer to deliver the results.

'I was asked to select one winner today. A dish that best replicated mine in terms of taste and aroma. To be frank, this wasn't an easy task at all. All of you have done really well and produced amazing dishes that are very similar to my own. But one dish in particular stood out to me. By tasting the dish, I could tell that the chefs worked meticulously and patiently to reproduce my culinary style. So, the winning team today is . . . Chef Dustin and Chef Maya. Please join us at the front,' he said.

Maya couldn't believe her ears. Dustin was probably destined to be a chef if he could win despite having a weak link like her on his team. She could hear Rohan cheering loudly from the sidelines. She turned to look at him and he was beaming. He gave her two thumbs up and urged her to move forward towards Chef Daniel. Dustin and Maya walked to the front of the foyer. Chef Daniel shook their hands and handed them a signed copy of his latest cookbook titled *Exploring Malaysian Culinary Gems*.

'Congratulations! You both did really well,' he said to them.

'Chef Daniel, I was completely useless. Dustin here is the one who did virtually everything. I spent half the time trying to peel ginger,' admitted Maya, sheepishly.

Chef Daniel laughed and said, 'I appreciate your honesty. Well done, Dustin. You showed great potential today. Keep it up.'

'Thank you, Chef. If you don't mind, could I ask you some questions about becoming a chef? Over coffee maybe? My treat,' Dustin said, flashing his charming, pearly white smile.

'Sure, I'm not in a hurry. Let's talk after this event.'

The three of them stood for photos as Maestro's student magazine photographer clicked pictures of them for the following month's issue. Once the event ended, the crowd around the foyer started to disperse. Dustin turned to Maya and said, 'Thank you, Maya. For today . . . for everything. And as promised, this is for you.'

He handed the signed copy of Chef Daniel's book to Maya.

She laughed and said, 'Dustin, you know very well that this book is better off with you. I've finally found a book that I'm not at all interested in reading.'

Dustin smiled and said, 'Thanks again, Maya.'

'You're welcome. Now go already! As I remember, you promised Chef Daniel a cup of coffee,' she replied.

Dustin waved goodbye and joined Chef Daniel for their chat. Maya walked over to Rohan who was patiently waiting for her at the edge of the foyer.

'You didn't have to stand around for the whole thing, you know,' she said.

'I know. But I'm glad I did, though.'

'Really?'

'Yeah, we finally found the one thing that you completely and utterly suck at,' he replied, trying hard to suppress his laughter.

Maya just rolled her eyes and ruffled Rohan's hair in retaliation. She was glad to finally have her best friend back.

Chapter 19

For the first time in weeks, Maya and Rohan were having lunch together in the dorm café. Maya texted Mei to join her. She didn't tell Mei about her having made up with Rohan. She wanted it to be a surprise. Mei walked into the café wearing a pair of well-fitting jeans and a crop top. She had accessorized the outfit with dramatic earrings, chunky gold bangles, and a bold red lip. Mei looked around the café trying to spot Maya. When she saw Maya and Rohan sitting together and chatting jovially, her relief was palpable.

She ran over to them and practically yelled, 'Finally! Thank you for putting an end to World War III.'

Maya and Rohan laughed at Mei's dramatic entry.

'Was it really that bad?' Maya asked.

'YES! It was horrible seeing you guys fight and I hated being caught in the middle of all that drama. Plus, Rohan looked like a sad puppy the whole time, which was both upsetting and annoying,' Mei said as she settled down beside Maya.

'I did not,' Rohan protested. 'I just . . . missed us hanging out,' he added, looking over at Maya.

'I missed us hanging out too,' Maya replied feeling glad that they were finally putting that stupid fight behind them.

'Something tells me Rohan missed you a little extra,' Mei teased as she winked at Maya.

Rohan's cheeks reddened. 'Well . . . yeah . . . I missed Maya's company. It's not a crime to miss your friends, right? In fact, I'm pretty sure it's normal human behaviour. Now can we please drop it?'

Maya sensed Rohan's discomfort, so she distracted Mei with her favourite topic of conversation: fashion.

'Mei, you look amazing! Are those earrings new?' Maya asked, partly to change the subject, but mostly because she truly was in awe of Mei's overall look.

'Thanks. I was taking pictures by the pool for my Insta account. And yes, these earrings are new,' Mei replied excitedly. 'This new jewellery company called Starry Night reached out to me and offered to pay me to promote their products on Insta. I told them to send a few samples and if I liked them, I'd style some looks and post them online. They sent a few pieces over yesterday and I'm obsessed. These are my favourite,' she said pointing at her gold, triangular earrings with feather dangle pieces on each of them.

'That's great, Mei. Can I see the pics you took?' Maya asked.

Mei whipped out her phone and opened her gallery. She then handed it over to Maya and Rohan.

'These look really good,' said Rohan, impressed by Mei's selfie skills.

'Thanks. The lighting by the pool is on point today. I can't wait to post these pics later. Hashtag sponsored post,' Mei replied.

'Hashtag my friend is a fashion influencer,' Maya said.

'Hashtag jeans rock,' Rohan added.

'In this context, they do, my friend, they really do,' Mei agreed.

Maya returned Mei's phone and couldn't help but ask, 'So . . . does this mean "Totally Mei" is back for good?'

Mei smiled. 'Yeah. Thanks to you guys, I've decided to give "Totally Mei" a fighting chance. If I give up before I even get started, I'll regret it for the rest of my life. I have two years to graduate, right? A lot can happen in two years. We'll see where this journey goes.' Starting to get a little teary-eyed, she added, 'If you guys have so much faith in "Totally Mei", then I should too.'

'Mei, we disagree on a lot of things. Like who would survive a zombie apocalypse—'

'Oh my God, Rohan, just let it go. You wouldn't stand a chance,' Mei retorted.

'What about me?' Maya cut in, feeling a little left out.

'Oh, you'll survive, obviously. I've got your back,' Mei said, winking at Maya cheekily.

Rohan snickered and shook his head. 'We argue about a lot of stuff. But one thing that needs no debate is the fact that you're super talented, Mei. We're only in our first year of uni and you're already getting offers left and right from brands. Just keep doing what you're doing. You're defo gonna make it big one day,' Rohan replied.

'Aww, you're going to make me cry,' Mei said as she dramatically fanned her eyes, desperately trying to prevent her mascara from running. 'Thanks for the pep talk. You're pretty good at this, you know? I think you've got potential to be a motivational speaker.'

'Right. Who the hell would pay to hear my pep talks? The only reason you two listen is 'cos it's FOC.'

Mei and Maya laughed, nodding in agreement.

'Well, whatever happens, we're here for you, Mei,' Maya replied, wrapping her arms around Mei to give her the sort of comforting hug that only best friends can offer. After that, they had lunch and caramel frappés while chatting about anything and everything. Maya updated Rohan about what happened with Dustin and how he was now on a quest to find his passion.

Rohan told them about his online tutoring that was still going strong. He had gotten himself a few new students and was thinking of venturing into teaching mathematics as well.

'Rohan, if you can wrap your head around the math and all the formulas in Mr Park's class, you can definitely teach O-Level mathematics. Go for it!' Mei encouraged him.

'Thanks, Mei. I've finally saved enough to buy a plane ticket back home for the semester break. My parents were shocked when I told them. I think my mum almost cried,' he shared excitedly.

'That's awesome! You can finally go and annoy your sisters for a change,' Mei teased.

Rohan rolled his eyes. 'Yeah, yeah, whatever. You guys are annoying as hell, too.'

This was followed by a chorus of boos from the girls. Mei went on to tell them about the collaborations she had planned for her Instagram account. Over the semester, Mei's account had blown up and her follower count was up to 10,500. She connected with a few other Malaysian fashion influencers over social media, and they planned to meet up for a joint photo shoot over the semester break. Most of them were from Penang, so they decided to shoot at popular tourist attractions across the island.

'Babe, come stay with me. I'll show you around and take you to all the best makan places,' Maya said excitedly.

'That's the plan,' Mei replied.

They continued chatting for over two hours before Maya got a call from her mum. 'Hi Mum . . . hello . . . hellooo . . . can you hear me? Hold on, let me go outside.' Maya got up and walked out of the café looking for a spot with better reception. The café had a lot of good things on its menu, but cell service wasn't one of them.

'So . . . when are you gonna tell her?' asked Mei.

'There's nothing to tell,' said Rohan, as he took a sip of his frappé, avoiding eye contact with Mei.

'Are you kidding me? There's A LOT to tell,' Mei exclaimed.

'Mei, just forget what I told you the other day, okay? I wasn't thinking straight and I blurted out some nonsense—'

'Nonsense? No, Rohan. You saying you have nothing to tell Maya, now that's nonsense. Just tell her what you told me.'

'I can't, okay? Just drop it.'

Mei snickered. 'You know what, Rohan. Don't tell her. Just bury it inside and stay silent forever. But when another Dustin comes along, and another will come along, don't expect Maya to read your mind.'

Rohan was about to say something when Maya walked back over to their table.

'Sorry, guys, the signal in here is terrible. What are you guys talking about anyway?' Maya asked.

'Nothing,' said Rohan quickly before Mei had a chance to butt in.

'Another one of your usual debates?' Maya asked curiously.

'Yeah, as usual, Rohan's wrong and he's just too blind to see it,' Mei replied.

Rohan glared at her. 'And as usual, Mei always has to be right. It's your way or the highway, right?'

'In this case, it is. Cause your way is stupid. But if you insist on being an idiot, I can't stop you. All right, guys, I've got to run. See you later,' Mei said before leaving the café for another mini photoshoot in the rooftop garden with a different pair of earrings.

'Geez! That was intense. Your debates are seriously next level. What was it even about? Were you two arguing about those Marvel movies again?'

'Yeah . . . something like that,' Rohan replied with a weak smile.

Chapter 20

The remainder of the semester flew by in a haze of tests and assignments. Soon, they were done with their finals and were all set to enjoy their semester break. Rohan was excited to head home after the longest year of his life. After their usual post-exam celebrations over good food and sweet frappés, Rohan packed his bags and headed to the airport to catch the red-eye back to Delhi.

Over the course of the semester, he had slowly accumulated things to bring home for his family. Local chocolates and sweets for his sisters, interesting spice mixes and batik shawls for his mum, and Malaysian stamps for his dad who was an avid collector. He dozed off on the flight and before he knew it, the plane was landing at New Delhi airport. After collecting his bags, he stepped out of the airport and inhaled the Delhi air after ages. It smelled like home. He booked an Uber, and on the ride home, he relished the sights and sounds of his hometown that he used to take for granted.

A half hour later, he was standing in front of an apartment complex, with bags in both hands. As he trudged up the stairs to the sixth floor, lugging his large suitcase and backpack, Rohan started to miss the elevators in Maestro. After much struggle, he managed to heave his luggage onto the sixth-floor landing and knocked on the door of the third apartment to the right.

Mrs Das's face lit up as she opened the door and saw Rohan. She gave him a tight hug and showered kisses all over his face.

'Welcome home, beta,' she said as she helped him bring his things inside. Their humble apartment, although a tad cramped for six people, was warm and inviting. The familiar aroma of incense and spices hit Rohan as he walked in. He was finally back home.

That night, Mrs Das made exactly what Rohan was craving: chapatis and rajma. He would groan when his mum prepared this meal at home when he was younger, having eaten so much of it over the course of his life, but a year away from home really made him appreciate his mum's cooking. Nasi lemak was great, but nothing compared to the soft, fluffy chapatis Mrs Das whipped up with such ease. His sister, Sheela, who was helping Mrs Das roll out the balls of dough, wasn't quite as adept at it as her mum. Rohan pointed this out, adding that she should sharpen her chapati-making skills if she wanted to land a rich husband someday and ducked just in time as she swung the rolling pin at his head. He had a knack for annoying Sheela, an innate ability most brothers possessed.

The next few days were spent visiting relatives, catching up with old school friends, and eating more home-cooked food. After the stress of assignments and exams, Rohan really appreciated this blissful downtime until his dad sat him down one day for one of his serious father-son talks over chai.

'Rohan, Mummy told me you got your results today,' Mr Das started as he dunked a digestive biscuit in his chai.

'Yes, Papa. I passed all my papers,' Rohan shared excitedly as he poured himself a cuppa. As much as he enjoyed cold frappés, nothing could compare to the soothing powers of a steaming cup of masala chai.

'What's your CGPA currently?' his dad asked, before popping the chai-soaked biscuit into his mouth.

'Oh . . . it's about 3.5 right now,' Rohan nervously sipped on his chai. He didn't like where the conversation was headed.

'That's okay, but you should try to do better, beta. I spoke to Mr Sharma, the assistant manager at ABC International Bank, and he said they usually hire candidates with a CGPA of 3.8 or above. That's a good bank, you know. Mr Sharma's daughter also joined the bank recently, Jaipur branch, and she got a high starting salary. I heard bonuses are also very good. You need better grades to land a good bank job like that,' Mr Das advised sternly.

Rohan was at a loss for words. He was actually quite proud of himself for getting through all his papers that semester, especially corporate finance, the killer paper with a failing rate of 60 per cent. He contemplated whether to bring this up but felt that his dad was more of a glass-half-full kind of guy when it came to these things and would almost certainly point out that 40 per cent passed, which meant the paper was doable.

Biting his tongue, he chose to just nod and assure his dad that he would work harder to improve his grades. Mr Das gave his son a pat on the back and continued to enjoy his chai and biscuits. Rohan excused himself, leaving his beloved masala chai unfinished, and went to his room. As he shut the door, wondering how he was ever going to meet his dad's high expectations, his phone pinged. It was Maya. She sent him a funny meme featuring cute penguins that made him smile.

*LOL. How is your timing so impeccable? Thanks for the much-needed
pick-me-up!*

Seconds later, his phone pinged again. *U okay?*

Yeah . . . just some stuff with my dad.

Ping. *FaceTime tonight?*

Sure, see you then.

Rohan felt the heavy weight of expectations ease a little,
knowing that he had someone to share it with. He pocketed
his phone and headed to the kitchen, suddenly feeling curious
about what they would be having for dinner.

* * *

Maya flew back to Penang the day after their finals. Mei was set
to join her the following week. The first week of the semester
break was blissful. Her mum took the week off and they spent
their days frequenting cafés, shopping, and watching movies
at the local cinema. Maya was used to people doing a double
take when she was out and about with Mrs Joseph. Most people
were often surprised to hear that the big-boned, blonde British
woman was her mum. However, any doubt or confusion
instantly vanished when people got to know them, because
Maya had so clearly inherited her mum's beautiful laugh and
warm personality.

Maya had missed her mum terribly while she was in Maestro,
especially when she'd had that big fight with Rohan. She used to
tell her mum everything when she was in high school, but now
that she was away from home, she didn't want to worry her mum
unnecessarily. Things were already tense at home between her
parents because of her career choice and Maya didn't want to
make things more difficult for her mum. She was glad to finally
be back home, spending precious quality time with Mrs Joseph.

When they were having lunch at a local café one day, Maya finally told her mum about what had happened with Susan Tan. Somewhat taken aback, Mrs Joseph set her fork down before replying, 'I can't believe they allow that woman to teach aspiring writers. How is poor Esther doing?'

'She's doing all right. I spoke to her last week, and she seemed happy. Her business classes are quite interesting, and she's grown to like them,' Maya replied before taking a sip of her rose iced latte. 'To be honest . . . I almost gave up on writing. If it weren't for Rohan, I don't think I would've found it in myself to ever write again.'

Mrs Joseph's eyes twinkled as she smiled at her beautiful daughter. 'Seems like you've found yourself a keeper.'

'What? No, it's not like that. He's just a really good friend,' said Maya, self-consciously tucking her hair behind her ear.

'Either way, I'm glad you're surrounded by supportive people who can lift your spirits when you're feeling low, my dear. That's worth more than all the riches in the world.'

Mrs Joseph reached across the table and gave her daughter's hand a little squeeze. Maya smiled and shook her head. Her mum was always dropping pearls of wisdom and as cheesy as it sounded, Maya appreciated every word.

After a week of mother-daughter bonding, it was time for Mei to join the Joseph household. Maya and her mum picked up Mei from Penang International Airport on a Sunday afternoon. The airport was bustling with people as travellers zoomed in and out of the airport, wheeling large suitcases. This wasn't surprising given Penang's reputation as a popular tourist attraction and food haven. Mrs Joseph pulled up in the arrival lane and shortly after, Maya spotted Mei with her huge, hot pink suitcase, walking out of the airport wearing sweats and a hoodie. Maya got out and ran towards Mei, almost knocking her down with the force of her hug. After some struggle, the girls managed to wrestle the suitcase into the boot before sitting together at the back of the car. As they headed back to Maya's house, the girls excitedly planned out their next fortnight together.

'I've got a shoot with the girls tomorrow. After that, I'm free. What shall we do?' Mei asked.

'I'll show you around, there are tons of cool cafés we can check out,' Maya replied excitedly.

'Keep yourselves free tomorrow night, girls. I'll be cooking dinner,' Mrs Joseph interjected.

'Don't worry, Mum, I haven't forgotten. My mum's making all her signature dishes, Mei: garlic naan, lamb rogan josh, chicken tikka, bhindi masala, and bread and butter pudding. Honestly, I've been more excited about this dinner than I've been about your arrival,' Maya grinned from ear to ear.

'Maya!' Mrs Joseph scolded. Mei rolled her eyes and punched her best friend who evaded just in time.

'Just kidding. I'm glad you're finally here, bestie,' Maya hugged Mei and gave her a big, slobbery kiss on the cheek.

'Eugh, stop,' Mei protested, pulling away and wiping her cheek on her sleeve. 'Rohan is gonna freak out when he finds out that he's missing such an amazing feast.'

'Yes, Maya told me about him,' Mrs Joseph said with a knowing smile that Maya chose to ignore before adding, 'Hopefully he can visit us next time.'

'Aunty, did you learn Indian cooking after you got married? Maya always raves about your cooking. Every time we eat Indian food, she always says that it pales in comparison to your cooking.'

In the rear-view mirror, Mei could see Mrs Joseph smiling and her pale cheeks turning red. 'Oh, Maya is exaggerating. I'm a decent home cook at best. And yes, dear, I learned to cook Indian food after Maya's dad and I got married. His mother was a fantastic cook and teacher, so I picked up a lot from her. She was a saint.

One day, when I was particularly homesick, she made me fish and chips to cheer me up. Can you imagine? She had never cooked anything but Indian food her whole life, but she got young Maya to find a recipe online and followed it to a T. She used mustard oil to fry the fish and I swear, it was one of the best meals I've ever had. Sorry, girls . . . I'm going on and on,' Mrs Joseph laughed and waved dismissively, but Mei could tell that she was tearing up.

'It's okay, Mum. I like it when you talk about Paati. I miss her too,' Maya replied, giving her mum's shoulder a little squeeze. After battling Penang's notorious traffic jams for another half hour, they finally arrived home. Maya and her family stayed in a quiet, suburban area away from the city centre and their bungalow home was surrounded by lush greenery. From the wrought iron front gate, a stone walkway led up to the house. The garden area was full of plants with a variety of flowers. Mei recognized a few of them: rose, hibiscus, jasmine, and morning glory. The archway at the front porch boasted a majestic crown of fuchsia-pink bougainvillaea, which cascaded elegantly from above.

At the side of the house, a bronze garden table and a few chairs were arranged beneath a tall tree, offering shade and a place to sit. It reminded Mei of their usual spot in the campus cafeteria. From afar, Mei could hear the sounds of leaves rustling in the wind and birds chirping. Maya's home felt like a wonderful nature retreat after the concrete jungle of KL. Maya helped Mei with her luggage and they made their way upstairs. Mei would be staying in the guest room that was right next to Maya's room. After changing into comfy home wear, the girls spent most of the day hanging out in Maya's room.

'Babe, your bedroom is so you,' Mei had said the moment she walked in. The room was squarish with a queen-size bed against one wall and a gigantic bookshelf against the other. The bookshelf boasted copies of classic and contemporary titles, including Maya's favourite, *Pride and Prejudice*, which she had read cover-to-cover countless times. Next to the bed was a desk, above which was a window that overlooked the backyard. The window was open and the short, sheer curtains fluttered gently in the breeze. 'Welcome to my humble abode,' said Maya, her hands outstretched before crashing backwards into her comfy bed.

There was a knock on the door and Mrs Joseph appeared with a tray of cold lemonade and warm brownies for the girls. 'The weather is so hot nowadays; it's important to stay hydrated. Mei, make yourself at home. If you need anything, just let me know.'

'Thank you, aunty,' Mei replied, her eyes lighting up at the sight of the fudgy chocolate brownies.

Maya's mum placed the tray on Maya's desk and left, closing the door behind her. After enjoying the refreshments, they started going over the looks for Mei's shoot the next day. Mei tried on different pieces and styled them with funky, colourful accessories. For some extra inspiration, Mei raided Maya's closet and squealed in excitement when she came across a gorgeous cashmere turtleneck sweater hiding at the back.

'Maya, why haven't I seen you in this before? This is gorgeous,' Mei said.

'Babe, I wore that once, when I visited London in winter with my parents. I can't wear that here. Malaysia doesn't have turtleneck weather,' Maya retorted.

'Some sacrifices need to be made for the sake of fashion, darling,' Mei replied as she tried on the sweater that fitted her perfectly. She paired it with a miniskirt, sheer tights, ankle boots, chunky earrings and a gold watch.

'Mei, that looks amazing. I've had that sweater in my closet forever and I've never thought of styling it that way.'

'Thanks, babe. Can I borrow this for tomorrow's shoot?' Mei asked.

'Yeah, of course.'

Once Mei finalized her looks for the shoot and packed everything she needed, they spent the rest of the evening devouring more brownies and watching Netflix on Maya's laptop.

* * *

The next day, Mei's influencer friend picked her up and they were off to a whole-day shoot. While Mei spent the day moving from one location to the next, Maya did what she did best.

She made herself a cup of three-in-one coffee, an absolute must when the writing bug bit her, which usually was always. She brought her cup and laptop into the backyard and settled down at the patio table beneath their mystery tree. The tree had been there ever since she could remember. It didn't bear any fruit but had dense foliage that provided shade on hot days throughout the year. The tree did flower once a year, displaying delicate purple flowers. It was a sunny day, so Maya was extra grateful for the shade their mystery tree had to offer.

Soon after, the coffee started to work its magic and she wrote a new short story. Instinctively, she saved the story, attached it to an email, and sent it off to Rohan. In the email, she wrote a short note that read:

Wrote something new today, so I figured I'd forward it to my #1 fan. Hope you're having a good day with your family.

Maya took a break at lunchtime and devoured a packet of wonton noodles that her mum had bought from the wet market in the morning before making yet another cup of three-in-one coffee. She continued writing outside until sunset.

In that time, she managed to knock out another short story and do some research for what she liked to call her magnum opus—the sci-fi story she once submitted to Susan Tan—but a much longer version that she hoped would be published as a book someday when she was done. Between coffee runs and intense research, she took small breaks, mostly spent scrolling through 9GAG, looking at memes. She came across a particularly funny one, featuring penguins, and forwarded it to Rohan. Moments later, her phone pinged: *LOL! How is your timing so impeccable? Thanks for the much-needed pick-me-up!*

Pick-me-up? Was something wrong? Maya thought to herself before promptly replying: *U okay?*

Ping. *Yeah . . . just some stuff with my dad.*

Yikes. Their results had just been announced. Maya guessed that Mr Das wasn't too happy about Rohan's grades. Regardless, she knew all too well the heartache that came with a father's disapproval and she wouldn't wish it on her worst enemy, not even Susan Tan. Without thinking, her fingers flew across the keypad, typing out a response to her distressed friend.

FaceTime tonight?

Ping. *Sure, see you then.*

She attempted to continue her research, but was too worried about Rohan to concentrate, so she decided to call it a day. As she shut her laptop, a car pulled up in front of her house. Mei got down and waved goodbye to her friend.

'Hey, how did it go?' Maya asked, excitedly.

'Maya, it was amazing! We have to edit some of the pics before we post them tomorrow, but we were sharing Insta stories about the collab and shoot the whole day and the response has been wild. I can't wait to officially post our looks tomorrow,' Mei said before sitting down beside Maya and whipping out her iPhone to show her the pictures from the shoot.

'Mei, these are incredible. Your looks, the backdrop, everything is gorgeous. And you look so natural in the pictures, babe,' Maya praised as she scrolled through Mei's gallery.

'Thanks, Maya. I had so much fun. If anything, today really proved to me that fashion is where I belong.'

'That's amazing, Mei. I'm so happy for you,' Maya replied encouragingly as she gave Mei a hug.

'Girls, dinner will be ready soon,' Mrs Joseph called out.

'Okay, Mum. We'll go freshen up before the much-anticipated feast begins,' Maya said cheekily before dashing upstairs with Mei.

Half an hour later, the Josephs and Mei were seated for dinner. Mrs Joseph piled a tonne of food onto Mei's plate. Initially, Mei wasn't sure if she could finish everything, but after the first bite, she just couldn't get enough.

'Aunty, everything is so good, especially the lamb curry. It's the best I've ever had,' Mei gushed as she took a second helping.

'Thank you, Mei,' Mrs Joseph smiled.

'Yes, Hillary's lamb curry is very good. But cannot beat my mother's, lah,' Mr Joseph said as he laughed loudly.

'Appa, it's not a competition,' Maya reprimanded, feeling annoyed at her father.

'It's just a joke. Your curry is very nice, Hillary,' said Mr Joseph to his wife, who nodded with a weak smile on her face.

'Mei, I heard you had a photoshoot today. What was it for?' he asked curiously.

'Oh . . . I hope to be a stylist one day, so I started a social media account to promote my looks and build a following. My marketing lecturer was the one who encouraged me to start this whole thing. The shoot was a collaboration with another influencer, and we'll be posting different looks featuring sponsored accessories on Insta tomorrow,' Mei explained.

'Wow! Sounds like you have a whole business plan all thought out. And you're only in your first year?' Mr Joseph sounded quite impressed.

'Yeah, but I have a long way to go,' Mei said modestly.

'Nonsense. Mei's being humble. She has over 10,000 followers on Insta and so many girls DM her for fashion advice. She's on track to become a fashion icon,' Maya gushed like a proud mama.

'That's very impressive, Mei. Maya, you should learn from your friend here. After professional courses like medicine and engineering, business is the next best career track. It will give you something to fall back on if your writing career doesn't take off.'

Maya stopped eating. Even with her favourite lamb curry in front of her, she had suddenly lost her appetite.

'Uncle . . . the things we learn in business classes are mostly theory. They aren't always very practical. I think it's more important to have a skill to fall back on rather than a degree. Maya is a very talented writer, and her skill will take her very far, I'm sure of that,' Mei loyally defended Maya.

'I agree with you, Mei. Skills are important, but companies usually assess your skill level through paper qualifications, so, like it or not, a degree is important. With a business degree, you can work virtually anywhere. Not many companies are queueing up to hire English literature graduates,' said Mr Joseph, oblivious to the rising temperature in the room.

Maya shot out of her chair, livid. 'One day, when I'm a famous writer, don't you dare tell people I'm your daughter,' she said before storming off to her room.

She slammed her bedroom door shut and fell onto her bed, sobbing uncontrollably. As she reached out to her nightstand for a tissue, her phone came alive with a familiar sound.

Chapter 21

'Hey, can you hear M—Maya, are you crying? What's wrong?' Rohan asked when Maya answered his FaceTime call, still in tears.

'Hey,' Maya replied weakly, wiping her cheeks with a tissue.

'Maya, what happened? Are you okay?'

Maya was trying hard to hold it together but hearing Rohan's concerned voice opened the floodgates. She broke down and told Rohan what happened.

'I can't believe he said that,' Rohan replied, his anger towards Maya's father rising.

'Well, I can. He's always saying stupid shit like that.'

'I'm sorry, Maya. Parents can be . . .'

'Insensitive? Heartless? A pain in the ass?' Maya sniffed dolefully, reaching for another tissue to wipe her never-ending stream of tears.

'Yeah.' Rohan thought back to the conversation he'd had earlier with his father. 'Have you shown your dad any of your stories? Did you tell him that you got shortlisted for that writing competition?'

Maya snickered and replied, 'No. He's never shown any interest in my writing. I'm sure he'd just say more stupid shit that'll only upset me further.'

'Maybe you should show him your work. You can write, Maya. Your dad just has to read your stories to know it,' Rohan said.

'You're my friend; you have to say that,' Maya exclaimed.

'Maya, you can't keep doubting yourself all the time. Randos with no talent don't get shortlisted for a national level competition.'

'Well, my dad is convinced that a degree is more important than talent.'

'Do you agree?'

'Of course not!'

'Then that's all that matters. Remember how I told you that not everyone is going to like your writing and that's okay? Well, not everyone is going to like all your life choices either. If writing makes you happy, which it obviously does, then you have to learn to drown out the noise. Even if it's coming from your dad.'

Maya nodded as she blew her nose into a tissue.

'For what it's worth, Mei and I think you're amazing and we support you, no matter what,' Rohan added.

'Thanks, Rohan. That means a lot,' Maya replied, her eyes brimming again, touched by her best friends' unwavering support.

Just then, Mei opened the door and popped her head inside. 'Hey, you okay?'

'Yeah, I'm okay. Sorry I abandoned you at the dinner table,' Maya said, feeling a little embarrassed.

Mei waved her hand dismissively. 'Don't apologize, babe. What your dad said was so not cool. I'm surprised you didn't flip the table!'

'That would've made for one heck of a family dinner,' Rohan commented, waving at Mei from the computer screen.

Mei hopped onto the bed and the three of them continued chatting. Half an hour later, Mrs Joseph cracked open her daughter's bedroom door to check in on her. She heard Maya and her friends chatting and laughing about Mei's fashion mishap earlier that day at one of her shoot locations. Mrs Joseph smiled, feeling reassured that she didn't have to worry so much about Maya any more. Her daughter had good friends who helped her through tough times.

* * *

'Rohan, you're one of the smartest people in class. Corp finance was crazy, but you always managed to complete most of the tutorial questions on your own. And you were Mr Park's favourite,' Mei said when Rohan finally told them what happened with his dad.

Rohan's video was a little grainy, but they could clearly see how upset he was. He shrugged and said, 'Well, apparently it's not good enough for Mr Sharma, so I've got to try harder.'

'Rohan, at the risk of sounding cliché . . . there's so much more to life than good grades. Sure, working hard and doing your best is important, but beyond that, stressing about grades will get you nowhere. Your dad might not understand this, but it's important that you do. Just keep doing what you're doing, Rohan. Things will work out in the end,' Maya reassured him.

'Yeah. And I disagree with your dad, by the way,' Mei added. 'I don't think companies just look at grades when they hire people. Someone could have a 4.0 CGPA, but if they have a bad attitude or lack common sense, I wouldn't hire them. If you're worried about landing a job after graduation though, there are things you could do to beef up your résumé.'

'Like what?' Rohan asked, leaning forward curiously.

'Well, you could apply for internships at local banks or financial institutions. Maybe even join a club or two. Actually, that reminds me, the business club hosts a student entrepreneur contest every semester.' Mei had clearly piqued Rohan's interest, so she added, 'Basically, you design a new product and pitch it to a panel of investors. The top three pitches win a grant to get the ball rolling on their ideas. Something like that would look awesome on your résumé, Rohan.'

'Yeah, I think I'll give that a shot.'

'There are a lot of Mr Sharmas in the world. You've just got to drown out the noise,' Maya replied with a wink.

Rohan broke into a laugh. 'I guess I should take my own advice.'

They went on talking for another hour before bidding each other goodbye. Rohan could barely keep his eyes open, so he went straight to bed. The girls, on the other hand, continued chatting.

'You okay?' Mei asked, worried that Maya was still thinking about her father's hurtful words.

'Yeah, I'm okay. I was pretty upset, but Rohan gave me one of his pep talks and it kinda helped.'

'I bet it did,' Mei replied with a glint in her eyes.

'What?' Maya raised an eyebrow.

'Oh, nothing.'

'Mei, what are you not telling me?'

'I can't say,' Mei replied, gesturing that her lips were sealed.

'Babe, what is it? Just tell me already!'

'Fine! But only because Rohan might take it to the grave if I don't. A couple of months ago . . .'

* * *

TWO MONTHS AGO

Mei got a text from Rohan asking her to meet him in the rooftop garden after class. When she got there, she saw him sitting on one of the benches, staring into the distance.

'Hey, what's up? Why are we meeting here? Can't we go to the café and chat over coffee?' Mei asked, standing in front of Rohan, blocking his view of the city's skyline.

Rohan snapped out of his daze. 'Hey . . . yeah, we can go in a minute. But first, I've got to ask you something.'

Mei settled down beside Rohan. 'Okay . . . hit me.'

Rohan scratched his head, trying to find the right words. He had already managed to piss Maya off. He didn't want Mei to be upset with him as well. 'I know it's none of my business, but . . . what's the deal with Maya and Dustin? Are they . . . together?' Rohan looked straight ahead, avoiding eye contact with Mei. He was embarrassed to ask, but he just had to know.

Mei crossed her arms and arched her brow. 'Rohan, Maya's really upset with you and if she found out that I was dishing about her love life to you, she'd hate me too. Just go apologize to her and then you can ask her yourself.'

'Mei . . . what if she doesn't accept my apology? What if she doesn't want to be my friend any more?' Rohan tried hard to fight back tears. The thought of Maya not being a part of his life was too painful to even contemplate.

'This is Maya we're talking about. Sure she can be hot-tempered at times, but she doesn't just turn her back on people. Go and talk to her. I'm sure you guys can work it out,' Mei assured.

'You don't know that for sure, Mei. I just . . . I don't want to lose her, you know. I said some stupid stuff the other day and I'm afraid she hates me for it,' Rohan replied softly, looking down at his shoes. He wished he could take back his words. He would give anything to go back, to change things.

'Well, why did you say all those stupid things? For a smart guy, your choice of words was very, very far from smart. Heck, if you said those things to me, I'd be hella pissed too!' Mei exclaimed, throwing her hands up in the air.

'I don't know . . . I just couldn't stand seeing the two of them together . . . Dustin and his stupid pearly whites, so obviously flirting with Maya . . . he just rubs me the wrong way.'

'Why? You don't even know the guy, Rohan. You were so preachy and judgemental to Maya, saying that she barely knew Dustin, but I could say the same about you. You're hating him without knowing the first thing about him. What is it with you dudes, huh? Is it a male territorial thing? Maya is your friend, so no other guy can approach her? What, you think in some way, she's your property? Is that it?' Mei replied feeling frustrated about this stupid fight between her friends.

'No, Mei, it's not that—'

'Then, what is it, Rohan? Help me understand 'cos right now, I don't get you. Why were you such a jerk to Maya?' Mei demanded, wanting an answer for why her usually sweet friend acted like a colossal dickhead.

'Because Maya shouldn't be with Dustin, she should be with me,' Rohan blurted out, finally looking up at Mei, his eyes brimming with tears.

'Oh . . .' The witty and always-ready-with-a-comeback Mei was speechless. She'd figured that Rohan had acted the way he did because of his conservative upbringing. It didn't occur to her that he might be having feelings for Maya. But now that she knew, she felt like a blind fool for not seeing it sooner. Finally, Mei found her voice and her tone softened.

'So . . . you like Maya? Since when?' Mei asked, leaning in towards Rohan curiously.

'I don't know. I guess I've always sort of liked her. I just didn't realize it until Dustin started flirting with her. Seeing them together makes me want to punch something, you know?' Rohan clenched his fists and looked away.

'Rohan, you need to tell Maya,' Mei exclaimed excitedly.

'Isn't she with Dustin? I don't want to be the jerk who professes his feelings for someone who's already taken.'

'I don't know what to tell you, Rohan. Things are . . . complicated between Maya and Dustin. Even I don't know what's going on between them. It could be nothing. You need to apologize to Maya and tell her how you feel.'

'No, I can't Mei. If she doesn't feel the same way I'll lose her as a friend . . . I'll lose her forever. I don't think I could stand that.' Despite his best efforts to hold them back, teardrops started running down Rohan's cheeks. Feeling embarrassed, he quickly wiped them away with the back of his hand.

'Well, if you don't tell her, she'll never know how you feel. And one day, she'll get a boyfriend who isn't you and you'll hate yourself for it. She may feel the same way about you and not even know it. Just like you.'

'No. I shouldn't have said anything to you. Look, I just want things to go back to the way they were. That's all. Just forget what I said and let's go get some coffee.'

'But, Rohan—'

'Mei, please. Let's just go,' Rohan said, giving Mei a steely look. His tear-streaked face hardened as he stood up and walked to the elevator. Mei trailed behind him, burdened by the weight of this secret.

* * *

'Rohan has feelings for me?' repeated Maya, after Mei told her what had happened.

'Yes, but please don't tell him I told you. He'll never forgive me,' Mei pleaded.

Maya, suddenly at a loss for words, just nodded.

'So . . . do you feel the same way?'

Chapter 22

'I . . . I don't know what to say, Mei. It's just . . . all so sudden' Maya finally said, still reeling from the shock.

'Well, do you like him?' Mei asked.

'Of course I like him. It's Rohan, he's one of my best friends. But do I like like him? Honestly . . . I'm not sure.'

'Okay, no pressure. Just think about it. For what it's worth, I think you guys would make a great couple,' Mei said before retiring to the guest room. She figured Maya would need some time to digest the new information she had dumped on her.

For the next two weeks, Maya thought a lot about Rohan and what she would say to him when the new semester started. Mei didn't want to pry, so she avoided the topic altogether and pretended as though nothing had happened. During the day, the two girls would hang out, watch movies, go café hopping, and enjoy each other's company. At night, once Mei retired to bed, Maya's brain would kick into overdrive and she couldn't stop herself from thinking about Rohan.

A week later, Maya decided to clear her head and went to a nearby café with her laptop in hand. Mei, meanwhile, had a lunch date with a fellow fashion influencer. Maya was happy to see Mei networking and collaborating with other fashion enthusiasts, and quite frankly, she needed a little alone time to mull over this whole Rohan situation. Maya took the bus and got off at a stop in the city centre. From there, she strolled down to one of her favourite cafés: Glasshouse by Mel.

As the name suggested, the café adopted a glasshouse concept with floor-to-ceiling windows that let in loads of natural light. It was a two-storeyed café, popular for its drinks and desserts. Maya entered and was welcomed by a rush of cool air, courtesy of the air-conditioning.

She ordered a chocolate muffin and the house special, a caramel matcha iced latte, before making her way up to the second floor. The windows overlooked a park across the road and offered a beautiful view. Maya sat down at a table by the window and soon after, Mel, the café owner, herself brought her order.

'One muffin and our signature latte,' Mel announced chirpily.

The tall, slender woman was wearing a denim apron over a pair of jeans and a grey T-shirt. She was always in a good mood. Even when the café was crowded, she would always stop to offer her patrons a warm smile.

'Thanks, Mel.'

'My pleasure,' Mel replied. She was about to head downstairs when she suddenly remembered something and turned back. 'Maya, I wanted to tell you, we'll be closed next week. Reopening the following Monday. Just wanted to update my favourite customer. Later I'll update on social media also.'

'Thanks for letting me know, Mel. Is everything all right?'

'Oh, yes! I'm getting married next week.'

'Oh, wow, that's wonderful news. Congratulations, Mel! You must be really excited.'

'Sort of. I've been with my boyfriend for so long, sometimes it feels like we're already an old married couple,' Mel said with a hearty laugh.

'That's nice. Sounds like you guys were high school sweethearts,' Maya added, leaning in closer, hoping Mel would share more details. She was a real sucker for a love story.

'Yeah, we met in high school, but we didn't hit it off right away. We were friends for a long time before we got together. But I think it's better that way, you know? It feels nice to marry your best friend,' Mel said, coyly. 'Anyway, I'd better head downstairs. Enjoy your meal, Maya.'

Maya could have sworn there was a spring in Mel's step that wasn't there before. *I guess love does that to you,* Maya smiled to herself and dug into her chocolate muffin. Luckily, she was the only one upstairs, so she didn't have to pretend to be graceful. She just carried the delectable pastry off the plate and wolfed it down. As she sipped on her latte, she tried hard to distract herself by writing, but she kept thinking about what Mel had said: 'We were friends for a long time before we got together. But I think it's better that way, you know? It feels nice to marry your best friend.'

Just then, Maya heard a ping on her laptop. It was an email from Rohan. Her heart started racing. With a shaky finger, she clicked on the email. It was a reply to a story she had sent him a little while ago.

Hey Maya,

I just realized that I devoured your story but forgot to reply!

As always, the story was AMAZING!

When the hero died, I legit teared up. I know they're fictional characters, but somehow, you make them feel so real.

Eagerly awaiting your next story.

Your biggest fan,

Rohan

Maya's lips curled into a tender smile as she read Rohan's reply. She typed in Rohan's name in the search bar and all the emails they had sent to each other over the past year appeared. As she scrolled through their many email exchanges, she felt a warmth radiate throughout her body. Maya had sent him dozens of stories and he had read them all—every single one. He always wrote back to tell her how much he loved them.

That whole fiasco with Susan Tan had almost made Maya quit writing, but Rohan had helped her believe in herself again. In fact, Maya couldn't think of anyone else who believed in her as much as Rohan did. Some days, Maya would write stories just for fun. Not for an assignment. Not for a competition. But just because she had someone to share them with. As the words flowed out of her, she would think to herself, 'I can't wait to show this one to Rohan . . .'

Suddenly, things just clicked in Maya's brain. She knew exactly what she was going to say to Rohan. And she was going to tell him in the only way she knew how.

* * *

With just a few days left before the start of the new semester, Maya was on a flight back to KL. Mei, on the other hand, had left the week before to pay her family a visit. It took all of Maya's willpower not to tell Mei about her plan. She wanted to keep this between Rohan and herself. Maya proofread the story she was going to send Rohan for the gazillionth time. She wanted to make sure it was perfect. As soon as the plane landed, she emailed the story to Rohan with the message: *This one's for you.*

After collecting her luggage, Maya took a cab to Maestro. There wasn't any traffic, but Maya felt that the journey back to campus was excruciatingly long. After thirty minutes, the cab driver pulled up in front of Maestro. Maya paid the driver and hurried through campus to the dorm. She went up to her floor, chucked her bags in her room, and headed up to the rooftop garden. The elevator doors opened and there he was.

Rohan was sitting on their usual bench, gazing at the KL skyline.

'You came,' Maya said from afar.

Rohan turned around, a smile erupting on his face when he saw Maya. He stood up and faced her, wanting to close the distance between them, but his legs seemed to have forgotten how to move.

'Yeah, I read your story, our story.' He took out his phone from his pocket and read aloud an excerpt from it.

M now knew her best friend had feelings for her. This changed everything. Somehow, the world looked a little different than it had before, and there was no going back.

She had thought long and hard about what she would say to her friend, but words never seemed enough when it came to matters of the heart. At last, she decided to meet him at their usual spot. The rooftop garden where they spent many hours looking out at the sunset and chatting about everything and nothing at all. Yes, it felt right to do this there.

So, she hopped onto a plane and made her way back to where it all began. The pilot couldn't fly the thing fast enough, but she waited patiently, all the while wondering how this would go. As the wheels of the plane made contact with KL soil, she turned on her phone and emailed the story to him, grabbed her bags, and ran faster than she had ever done in her life.

Finally, she was there. She took the elevator up and when the doors opened, he was there waiting for her. She smiled and said . . .

'So . . . Mei told you, huh?' Rohan asked sheepishly.

'Yeah, she did. She thought you'd never tell me otherwise.'

'This isn't how I wanted you to find out, but now that you know . . . how does the story end?'

In answer to his question, Maya did what Rohan was aching to do. She walked over to him and took his hand. Rohan's heart was pounding and he had to remind himself to breathe. He recognized the sweet, familiar scent of Maya's perfume. He had missed that scent. In fact, he had missed everything about Maya. Their eyes locked and their fingers intertwined. Maya leaned forward and gently kissed Rohan on the lips. He put his arms around her and drew her closer into a warm embrace.

Her first kiss. It was everything Maya had imagined it would be and then some. All the romance novels she had ever read didn't do justice to how magical this moment actually was.

'Wow,' said Rohan, as their lips parted. 'Does this mean you feel the same way?' he asked hesitantly.

Maya couldn't help but laugh. 'Yes, Rohan, I like you too.'

Rohan had the biggest smile plastered on his face. He picked up Maya and spun her around. 'Remind me to thank Mei when we see her,' he said excitedly.

'I'm pretty sure she'll remind you herself. By the way, do you have any plans later?'

Rohan put her down and answered, 'No, why?'

'Good. We're going out on our first date.'

Rohan smiled coyly and looked into her eyes in a way he never had before. It sent chills down Maya's spine. He tucked a stray hair behind her ear and said, 'The first of many, I hope.' Then he kissed her again, with the city skyline bearing witness.

* * *

Later that evening, Maya planned a surprise for Rohan. She gave him a box, with strict instructions to open it only when he was getting ready for the evening. Rohan obliged and at half past six, he opened the mystery box to reveal a sky blue kurta top with white beadwork around the collar and a pair of white leggings. Feeling more than a little intrigued, he put on the outfit before heading down to meet Maya. As Rohan made his way to the pool where they had agreed to meet, he caught sight of Maya from a distance and stopped in his tracks.

She was wearing a blue chiffon sari that perfectly matched Rohan's kurta. Maya had had no idea how to wear a sari, but with the help of countless YouTube videos and a bucketload of safety pins, she had managed to drape the five-metre chiffon material around her body in the nick of time. Glowing in the sunlight, with her sari pallu fluttering in the gentle breeze, Maya looked so achingly beautiful that Rohan forgot how to breathe. Once he recalled how to perform this vital exercise, he hurried towards Maya, not wanting to be apart from her any longer.

'You look amazing,' he said as he approached her. Maya smiled coyly before taking his hand and whisking him away on their first official date.

First, they went to a Hindu temple nearby, hence their traditional attire. Rohan wasn't particularly religious, but he did miss going to the temple with his family on weekends. He loved the calm atmosphere that places of worship offered, a retreat from all the craziness of life. He also admired the intricate architecture. Growing up in a Hindu family, he had only ever visited Hindu temples all his life. During his time in Malaysia, however, he had visited beautiful churches, pagodas, and mosques on his solo adventures around KL, which gave him a new-found appreciation for architecture.

They removed their shoes and entered the temple. Maya, who was a Christian, followed Rohan's lead. They washed their feet, purchased a prayer ticket from the counter and presented it to the priest who went on to perform prayers to Lord Ganesha. Maya admired the way they had beautifully decorated the statue of Ganesha with silk cloth and garlands of fresh flowers. After praying, they dabbed a tiny bit of *vibhuti* (sacred ash) onto their foreheads before sitting down in a quiet corner and sharing the banana that the priest handed to them. They each took half and savoured the sense of peace that the temple offered. After a while, they slowly made their way out.

On the Grab ride to Taj Palace, an Indian restaurant in Bangsar that apparently served the best biryani in town, Rohan reached for Maya's hand and they interlaced their fingers. He looked at her in the intense way he had done back at the rooftop garden and Maya's heart started to race.

'Thank you for today, Maya.'

'You should be thanking Mei. If she hadn't blabbed, you'd still be silently pining for me, and I'd still be hopelessly oblivious.'

Rohan nodded and took a selfie of them holding hands. He sent the picture to Mei with the message: *Thanks for blabbing, Cupid. Maya's bringing me out for biryani. Don't be jealous, OK? HAHAHA!*

A moment later, his phone pinged.

FINALLY! You owe me one, bro!

Rohan showed Maya the message and she cracked up.

'Mei is sooo gonna hold you to that!'

'Oh yeah, I'm screwed. But it's totally worth it,' Rohan replied as he lay his head back on the headrest and looked longingly into Maya's eyes.

Chapter 23

'Maya, I've been looking everywhere for you,' Dustin exclaimed as he approached the three musketeers at the campus cafeteria. As usual, they were at their spot under the tree. It was a week since the inception of YaRo—the playful amalgamation of Maya and Rohan by Mei—and the three of them were enjoying a blissful lunch, happy to be back on campus in each other's company.

'Hey, Dustin! How are you?' Maya replied. Dustin joined the gang and they chatted for a bit before he revealed the real reason he'd been looking for Maya.

'You're leaving?' Maya asked in shock. 'Why?'

'I'm switching to a culinary arts programme.'

Maya nodded slowly as she processed this new information. 'Good for you, Dustin. I'm sad to see you go, but it's great that you're pursuing your passion.'

'Yeah, six months ago, I didn't even realize I liked cooking and now I'm going into culinary arts. It's crazy how things work out sometimes.' Dustin ran his hand through his hair with a contented smile on his face. 'Anyway, I wanted to say thank you, Maya. If it weren't for you, I wouldn't have started exploring my interests and I defo wouldn't have discovered my love for cooking.' Rohan shifted in his seat, a little uncomfortable with this heart-to-heart between Maya and Dustin. Mei, who noticed Rohan's unease, pursed her lips, trying hard not to laugh.

Maya was surprised to see the usually light-hearted Dustin being sentimental and dewy-eyed. But that lasted less than a minute before he said, 'You know what this means, right? If people get food poisoning from my cooking, it's on you.' In his usual fashion, he flashed his pearly whites and winked.

Maya rolled her eyes and replied, 'As if. By the way, which uni are you going to?'

'Pinnacle U in Cyberjaya.'

'Oh, I know someone who goes there,' Maya replied excitedly.

'Nice. You've got to introduce us sometime. Oh, I almost forgot,' Dustin said before rummaging through his bag for something. He took out a box that had an illustration of the sun rising over mountains and the words 'The Sunrise Café' arching above it. He gave the box to Maya. She opened it, revealing a slice of cheesecake and a plastic fork inside. 'Just a little something to say thank you.'

Rohan peered inside curiously, quietly wondering whether he should have gotten Maya something to mark the start of their relationship.

Maya took a bite of the cheesecake, and it was just as yummy as it had been the other day. She passed the box to Rohan, urging him to give it a try. He smiled and took a bite before passing it along to Mei.

'Nice, right? I pestered the owner into telling me their secret ingredient: lemon zest. It really enhances the tanginess of the cream cheese,' Dustin shared enthusiastically.

'Well, it's definitely yummy. And something tells me you're going to do great in culinary arts,' Maya replied with a wink.

As Dustin bid them farewell, Maya grabbed her phone and after checking with Esther, shared her contact details with him. She had a feeling the two of them would hit it off.

* * *

Maya, Rohan, and Mei were officially second years. No longer wet behind the ears like they once were, they moved around campus with a quiet confidence. They knew Maestro like the back of their hand—all the shortcuts, good hangout places and spots with good phone signal. Maya didn't have any shared classes with her buddies that year, but that didn't stop her from hanging out with Mei and Rohan at every possible moment outside of class. As usual, they studied together, ate together, and took long walks around campus together (not to mention Maya and Rohan's weekly dates).

One day, between classes, the gang was enjoying lunch at the campus cafeteria when a bubbly Malay girl wearing jeans, a flowy long top, and a floral headscarf approached them at their favourite spot.

'Hey, guys. I'm Yati. I just wanted to let you know that the business club is hosting a contest called "Maestro's Next Top Entrepreneur" this semester. Here's a flyer with all the details. If you're interested in joining, just text us at the number listed below,' she explained, smiling cheerfully as she handed Rohan an attractive A4 flyer before heading over to the next table.

'Babes, this was the contest I was telling you about,' Mei said excitedly. The three of them huddled together to pore over the flyer.

Maestro Business School proudly presents
MAESTRO'S NEXT TOP ENTREPRENEUR

Do you have the next big business idea? Believe you have what it takes to go all the way? Pitch your idea and stand a chance to win RM 5,000 to kickstart your entrepreneurial journey!

You can join on your own or as teams of 2 or 3. Students of all faculties are welcome. In fact, we encourage cross-faculty collaborations for a more well-rounded pitch!
Good luck, future entrepreneurs!

'Guys, maybe we can join this thing together. Mei, this would look really good on your résumé too,' Maya suggested.

'That's a great idea, M,' Rohan replied. Having wanted a special nickname for Maya that only he used, Rohan had taken to calling her M. 'We just need to come up with a killer product idea,' he added.

'I think I might just have one,' Mei said cheekily before taking a big swig of her iced mocha.

* * *

Over the next few weeks, they worked on a product pitch. Mei had a great idea—a fashionable pet collar with a built-in GPS tracker, inspired by Cocoa. They were still in touch with Kak Lina who had told them that Cocoa liked to go *jalan jalan* and was often found strolling outside, exploring their neighbourhood. Being the smart kitty that she was, she always found her way back home, but Kak Lina was understandably worried that something could happen to Cocoa.

The three of them used their unique abilities to prepare the pitch. Mei sketched out some collar designs with bold colours and patterns, and they were certainly the most fashionable pet accessories Maya and Rohan had ever seen. Naturally, Maya came up with the product name, Fur Finders, and their tagline, 'Making missing pets a thing of the past.'

Rohan, using his wicked PowerPoint skills, created a stunning presentation. They were feeling pretty confident about their chances until Mei received an email from the organizing committee one afternoon.

'What the hell?' she exclaimed as they were having lunch together at the dorm café.

'What's wrong?' Rohan asked with a mouthful of noodles. Curry laksa was his new obsession.

'It's from Yati. She sent me the time and venue for the contest next week. Listen to this: *Please make sure to bring along your working prototype. Teams without one will be immediately disqualified!* she read aloud.

'What? I thought we were just pitching a concept. They need a prototype?' Maya asked in shock.

'That's crazy. They can't just spring this on us one week before the contest,' Rohan anxiously ran his hands through his hair, messing it up even further.

'Unless . . .' Mei went to the contest's webpage and scrolled down to the terms and conditions. It was extremely long and the font was tiny, which was why the gang had overlooked it before. 'Shit. It's here in the terms and conditions: ALL TEAMS NEED TO PRESENT A WORKING PROTOTYPE ALONG WITH THEIR

PRODUCT PITCHES. THIS IS TO ENCOURAGE PARTICIPANTS TO BE CREATIVE AND RESOURCEFUL IN THEIR ENTREPRENEURIAL JOURNEY. IN ADDITION, WE WANT TO ENSURE THAT ALL IDEAS PRESENTED ARE PRACTICAL. WE WILL NOT ENTERTAIN FANCIFUL IDEAS THAT HAVE NO MEANS OF BEING CREATED/PRODUCED. I can't believe we missed this.'

'Fuck.' Maya couldn't believe it. A moment ago, she was confident that they had a shot at winning this thing, but now, they could be disqualified. They inhaled their lunch at top speed and rushed upstairs to Maya's room to come up with a plan.

'Okay, what do we do?' Mei asked as she paced nervously back and forth.

'I don't know . . . maybe we can . . . contact some local manufacturers and ask them if they can produce a prototype for us?' Rohan suggested hesitantly.

'It's worth a try,' Maya replied as she started googling on her laptop.

An hour later, they had called a couple of garment manufacturers in KL, just to be laughed at. No one was willing to produce a single cat collar as a prototype without any guarantee of future orders. The last place they called seemed promising, but it would cost them a bomb to place a custom order.

'So that plan's a bust,' Rohan announced before crashing onto Maya's bed disappointedly.

Mei quickly moved on to plan B and started looking up cat collars online. 'Guys, look at this.' She showed them a basic white cat collar that was half off on price.

'Looks okay, but we can't just bring a regular collar, right? They want an actual prototype of our product,' Maya replied.

'Maybe we can get this collar and one of those cheap GPS tracker thingies for pets and put them together,' Mei suggested.

'Well . . . that might be our best bet right now,' Rohan replied after some consideration.

'The collar is pretty plain, but I can use Sharpies and rhinestones to jazz it up,' Mei added.

'Okay, let's do it,' Maya agreed.

Mei put in an express order and prayed that the items come on time. It was up to the delivery gods now.

* * *

The night before the contest, a package arrived for Mei. She tore the outer plastic wrapping and was relieved to see the collar and GPS tracker within. This godforsaken package had stressed them out so much. Although it had been shipped out immediately, it had somehow gotten stuck in a delivery hub for ages. They were on the verge of giving up when the package finally arrived.

With no time to spare, Mei got out her Sharpies and decorated the plain white collar with colourful swirls and floral themes before jazzing it up further with some sparkly rhinestones.

'Damn! Looks awesome, babe,' Maya gushed before Rohan attached the GPS tracker to the embellished collar. Now that they finally had a working prototype, they proceeded to practise and perfect their presentation.

At noon the next day, they waited anxiously outside tutorial room 205 in the business school building. All the groups had drawn lots and the three musketeers had got the last slot for their presentation. They spent the last two hours before their turn pacing the corridors, going through the presentation and scrolling their phones, trying to calm their nerves.

Finally, they were called into the room. The usual desks and chairs had been pushed back against the wall. Four tables were arranged in a row in the middle of the room for the judges who consisted of the business club committee members and Mr Matthews, their advising lecturer. Mr Matthews had a reputation of being kind of a hard-ass. His classes were notoriously difficult to ace, and he was generally hard to please.

'The floor is yours,' he said gesturing to the front of the room. Rohan hooked up his laptop to the projector and pulled up the Power Point presentation before nodding to Mei.

'Good afternoon, everyone. Before we get started, let me see a show of hands: How many of you have furry friends at home?' Mei began enthusiastically. Two of the four judges raised their hands. 'Lovely! I myself have a cutie at home by the name of Momo.' On cue, Rohan moved to the next slide featuring an adorable picture of Momo lying on her back, belly up, with her head tilted towards the camera.

The judges broke out in a chorus of awws in response to Momo's cuteness, except Mr Matthews who remained expressionless and aloof.

'Cute, isn't she? Well, we created our product with furry friends like her in mind. Let me elaborate.'

After fifteen minutes, the gang had run through their pitch with Maya taking over to explain their product name and tagline, and Rohan breaking down the details on costing, pricing, and expected profit. Thereafter, they unveiled their last-minute prototype and put it on a dog plushie before revealing a map on screen that reflected its real-time location.

'With Fur Finders, we can help thousands of people find and bring their precious friends back home, no matter what. Thank you,' Mei ended.

This was met with a weak applause from the judges.

Mr Matthews glanced around at the other judges with his enigmatic expression. 'Questions?'

'Yes,' replied one of the student judges. 'Thank you for your presentation, guys. Loved the slides and presentation style.' Maya, who was holding her breath, heaved a sigh of relief and smiled. 'But . . .' he continued, 'how is this different from a regular collar that has the pet owner's contact information?'

Maya's heart sank and she went completely blank.

Luckily, Rohan came to the rescue. 'Good question. With a collar like that, owners will only be able to find their pets if someone is kind enough to call them—in other words, we'll have no idea where our pets are until some good Samaritan comes along. But, with our product, you can immediately track your pet's location and find them.'

The student judge nodded approvingly and jotted down something on his scoring sheet. Maya discreetly gave Rohan a thumbs up before Mr Matthews decided to throw a question into the ring as well. 'Where did you source your materials?'

'Er . . . actually we ordered the collar and GPS tracker on Shopee,' answered Mei, hesitantly.

'So, couldn't I just order the collar and tracker myself? Wouldn't it be cheaper?' he queried with a raised eyebrow.

This time, Maya swooped in with a response: 'Actually, we're hoping to market this as fashionable pet collars. What we got online was a basic white collar and my teammate, Mei, actually decorated it herself.'

'So, the only thing you're adding is the drawing on the collars?'

The gang exchanged glances, unsure of how to answer.

'I'm sorry, guys, I don't think you have a solid product idea here. Sure, you're decorating the collars, but you're not really providing something new that people can't get elsewhere. From a consumer's perspective, I would much rather get a cheaper collar that does the exact same thing,' Mr Matthews added.

After that fiasco, the trio thanked the judges for their time and left the room. They hung around with the other participants, waiting for the judges to announce the winners, although they knew they stood no chance whatsoever. As expected, another team won with their movie night rental kit idea for college students.

'Ahh. I hate to admit it, but that does sound like a good idea,' conceded Maya.

Later that night, they ordered fast food and binged on it in Maya's room as they sulked over their loss. 'I'm sorry, guys. The collar was my stupid idea. The whole reason we joined this thing was so Rohan could bulk up his résumé and we have nothing to show for it,' said Mei, regretfully.

'Babe, it's not a stupid idea. I love the collar you decorated. If I had a pet, I would totally get it,' Maya assured.

'And Mei, we can all still add this to our résumés. There's no shame in participating in something and not winning. At least we tried,' Rohan added.

Mei smiled weakly and they continued eating their burgers and fries, huddled around Maya's laptop, watching a sitcom.

* * *

When they recovered from the disappointment of that day, Mei decided to post a picture of their collar on her page with the caption, Goodbye Fur Finders, along with a broken heart emoji. To her surprise, people started showing interest in it. At least a dozen people DM'ed her, asking about the collar and whether they could place an order for their furry babies.

'Are you serious?' Rohan asked in disbelief.

'Yeah! Some are requesting customized designs on the collar. There actually seems to be a market for this thing,' shared Mei, excitedly.

'What do you wanna do, Mei?' Maya asked.

'Let's sell these babies.'

Over the next few days, they started a new Instagram page for their Fur Finders and started getting orders right away. They put their savings together and bought a bunch of collars and GPS trackers. Mei added customized designs to the collar while Rohan and Maya attached the trackers and packed the orders. Once a week, they took a trip to the post office to ship the orders and treated themselves to frappés from the coffee shop next door. In the first month, they managed to sell seventy-five collars for 25 Ringgit apiece at a profit margin of 40 per cent.

On one particular Friday, Rohan and Mei were supposed to meet Maya back at their dorm unit to pack orders after their Digital Marketing class. Maya, who had started packing orders already, looked up at the wall clock. It was half past five in the evening. Even with their lecturer's tendency to go overtime, they should have been back by now.

She continued packing orders when she got a call from Mei. 'Hey, where are you guys?' she asked.

'Babe, something's happened. You've got to come down now,' Mei replied in a panic.

'What's going on, Mei? Are you guys okay?' Maya replied, grabbing her keys and rushing out the door.

'No time to explain. Just come down to the dorm café. Hurry!'

Maya rushed downstairs as all the worst-case scenarios played out in her head.

Calm down, Maya. You'll be of no use to anyone in a state of panic. Calm down. Whatever it is, the three of you will get through it together, she assured herself as the elevator descended at a snail's pace. After far too many stops, it finally reached the ground floor. She dashed out and ran to the café. Her heart pounding hard, she was caught off guard when her friends suddenly yelled 'Surprise!' in unison. It took a minute for Maya's nerves to settle down and to process what was going on.

One of the outdoor tables by the pool was sectioned off and the area was festooned with balloons. There was a two-tier, peach-coloured cake decorated with icing flowers and a sign that read 'Happy 21st Birthday!' on the table. Mei and Rohan popped out from under the table where they had been hiding, just as Maya was about to rush into the café.

'What's going on?' Maya asked, clearly confused.

Her two friends rushed forward and hugged her. 'Happy birthday, M!' said Rohan, before planting a kiss on the top of Maya's head.

'Happy birthday, bestie,' Mei added, following suit.

'But . . . my birthday isn't until tomorrow.'

'We know, but we wanted to surprise you. If we tried anything tomorrow, we were sure you'd catch on,' explained Mei.

After a few moments, Maya's shock turned into anger. 'I was so worried. Why would you do that?' she said, swatting her friends.

'Ahh! We're sorry. We didn't know how else to get you down here,' Mei shielded herself from Maya's wrath.

'You're turning twenty-one, M. Obviously we're gonna celebrate,' added Rohan. Mei then dragged Maya over to the table and planted a sparkler candle on the cake before lighting it. The candle burst into life, shooting glorious sparks in all directions. Rohan and Mei burst into a raucous, albeit out-of-tune, rendition of the Happy Birthday song. Her friends were amazing, but neither of them were blessed with a talent for singing.

Maya laughed merrily before squeezing her eyes shut to make a wish. *I wish we stay friends forever.* As soon as the sparkler candle died out, Maya cut out a slice of cake to feed her best friends. She lifted the piece smothered in frosting towards Rohan before smooshing it all over his face.

'That's what you get for tricking me,' said Maya mischievously before moving on to her next target. Mei made a run for it with Maya close behind her in hot pursuit. The girls ran around the pool until Maya managed to catch up with Mei and execute her revenge.

'Nooooooo!' Mei pleaded before Maya stuffed cake and frosting into her mouth and all over her face.

Not long after that, the tables turned and Maya found herself being chased by her friends who were determined to celebrate her birthday with a splash. After much commotion, and with passers-by stopping to stare at the three musketeers and their shenanigans, Rohan and Mei caught hold of Maya and pushed the birthday girl into the pool. The rest of the evening was spent drying off, eating cake and nasi lemak from the café, chatting and laughing so hard, they cried.

Just as they ordered another round of drinks, Mei's phone pinged. A few moments later, she squealed with delight.

'Dude, what happened?' Rohan asked.

'You guys aren't gonna believe this. Mr Matthews just placed an order for a Fur Finder,' she shrieked.

'No way,' exclaimed Maya, convinced that Mei was pulling another fast one.

'I'm serious,' said Mei, showing Maya her phone. It was a DM from @mattsinthehouse with a profile picture of Mr Matthews.

'Damn! He looks so much more chill in his profile pic. He's actually smiling.'

'Babe, is that what you're looking at? Read the message. His daughter follows me on Insta and wants a Fur Finder for their cat. She wants a customized collar with skull and bones.'

'Wow,' Rohan was speechless.

'Well, we couldn't impress Mr Matthews, but at least we managed to impress his daughter, right? I guess it's all about knowing your target demographic,' Mei joked.

'Best. Birthday. Ever.' announced Maya as they clinked their mason jars together in celebration.

Somewhere in the middle of all this craziness, Maya posted a picture of her friends with the balloons and cake in the background on Instagram with the caption: *My 21st came a day early. Couldn't have asked for a better way to kickstart this new phase of my life. Adulthood, here I come! #blessed.*

Years later, Maya would look back on that day fondly as one of her most memorable birthdays. Wishes may not always come true, but memories like that never fade.

Chapter 24

A year flew by in the blink of an eye. The three musketeers were about to begin their final semester at Maestro. Maya and Rohan's relationship, despite the occasional blowouts, was going strong. Mei, on the other hand, was happily single and rocking the fashion scene. Her Instagram account had grown exponentially after a major fashion influencer from Finland gave her a shoutout for her bold and wicked looks. Mei hit 100K followers during the semester break and tons of fashion companies and magazines were approaching her with job offers.

After the 'Maestro's Next Top Entrepreneur' contest, the gang had gone on to sell over fifteen hundred Fur Finders. Rohan added this to his résumé, along with his other extra-curricular activities, and potential employers definitely started noticing him. Apparently starting a small (and fairly successful) business despite the odds gave them more of a competitive edge than they realized. He ended up securing two internships to further bulk up his résumé and managed to get job offers at the end of both. Mr Das was so over the moon to hear about this that he even forgot to enquire about his son's current CGPA, which Rohan took as a very good sign.

Maya was writing, as always, and dreading the end of their time at Maestro. These past few years were like a dream. She was sad it had to end. If it were up to her, she would want the three of them to remain at Maestro for all eternity. Just eating nasi lemak and sipping on caramel frappés until the end of time. But, alas, every dream has to come to an end eventually.

Maya was dead set on making the most of their final semester. She came up with a plan and decided to bring it up at the dorm café on the first day of their last semester. With Malaysia Day coming up, the café had a promotion, offering 50 per cent off on all nasi lemak dishes for the entire week. The gang decided to milk this opportunity and order this beloved national dish every day.

Maya ordered nasi lemak ayam rempah, which came with a deep-fried chicken leg quarter, while the other two opted for nasi lemak sambal sotong that was served with tender, melt-in-your-mouth squid rings cooked in spicy sambal sauce. And of course, they ordered their usual frappés to complement the fiery nasi lemak. Maybe it was the realization that their days in Maestro were numbered, but Maya could have sworn that the frappés were sweeter and tastier than ever. After devouring her delicious nasi lemak (made even more delicious by its discounted price), Maya pitched her idea for 'Project 21 Events'.

'Guys, I wanted to talk to you about something.' She opened her backpack, took out the semester calendar that detailed all the important dates and events for that semester and laid it on the table in front of Rohan and Mei.

'What's this?' asked Mei.

'It's Maestro's semester calendar.'

'I didn't realize they even had such a thing.'

'Well, they do. I was going through it earlier and there are some pretty cool events lined up this semester.'

'You mean all the ones you've circled over here?' Mei asked in astonishment.

'That's a lot of circles, M,' Rohan added, a little concerned about where this was heading.

'Well, twenty-one in total, actually. I was thinking . . .'

'Oh no,' Mei muttered under her breath.

'. . . maybe we should attend these events. We always talk about going for these events, but we never do. It's our last chance to finally do it.'

'M . . . we each have different schedules, plus assignments and tests throughout the semester; some of them are even back-to-back in the same week. It would be impossible for us to attend all these events,' Rohan protested.

'Yeah, we have some killer subjects this semester. I don't wanna be a buzzkill, but this is basically suicide, babe,' added Mei, supporting Rohan's point.

'Okay,' Maya replied calmly. She had expected some resistance, so she had come prepared. She crossed her arms and continued, 'I'm open to negotiations.'

After much deliberation, the gang agreed to attend eight campus events, including the Maestro Ball at the end of the semester.

'All right, eight events it is,' Maya concluded before her friends could change their minds.

'Why do I get the feeling we just got played?' Mei asked, narrowing her eyes at Maya.

'Well, you two might be business students, but I know a thing or two about negotiating myself.'

'Touché,' Mei replied, tipping her imaginary hat to Maya. 'Wait, what's the first event again ah?'

'Murder Mystery Night,' replied Maya and Rohan in unison.

* * *

'I thought you said we had to dress up for this event,' said Maya, shooting daggers at Mei. 'We're literally the only ones here who are dressed up.'

'The flyer said it was a '20s-themed Murder Mystery Night. That means flapper dresses and feather headbands. Ask anyone,' Mei defended.

The three of them stood out like sore thumbs at Maestro's foyer area where all the other participants of the murder mystery event came clad in casual attire. They were drawing a lot of attention as the only ones dressed straight out of the 1920s. Maya was wearing a sequinned flapper dress with long pearl necklaces, vintage flapper shoes, and an eye-catching feathered headband. Rohan, who was holding her hand (partly to be romantic but mostly to keep her from clobbering Mei), was wearing an old-school, beige, pinstriped suit and a matching fedora. To complete the ensemble, he was holding a cane that Mei had insisted he needed to tie the whole look together.

Mei, on the other hand, was wearing a gold, flapper fringe dress with a white feather boa draped over her arms and held a long cigarette holder (minus the cigarette, of course). She also had on an extravagant headband with peacock feathers and pearls. Just then, a tall, skinny, dapperly dressed student in a black suit and tie walked onto the makeshift stage at the centre of the foyer to make an announcement.

'Hello, everyone. Welcome to the first ever Maestro University Murder Mystery Night. As uni students, we're constantly bombarded with assignments and exams. It's just stress, stress, and more stress. That is why the student council has organized this fun event tonight to help you de-stress and let loose,' said the guy, whom Maya now recognized as their student council president, Murali Kumar. This opening speech was met with a weak applause, mostly from other members of the student council. 'I see I'm not the only one who's dressed up for the occasion. The three of you at the back, I see you. Love your outfits.'

As if they hadn't been drawing enough attention as it is, now everyone was rubbernecking at them. Maya heard some snickering from a distance. She wanted nothing more than for the ground to open up and swallow her whole. Anything to spare her from this embarrassment.

'What he's wearing isn't even '20s themed. It's just a regular suit,' Maya whispered angrily to Rohan.

Rohan fought back a laugh and replied, 'Well, not everyone can pull off a fedora like I can, M.'

Maya laughed and playfully tugged down the fedora over his eyes. Just then, they heard a scream. Everyone rushed over to the open field and there, motionless on the ground, lay a girl in a flapper dress with what looked like ketchup smeared all over her chest and abdomen.

'Yikes! That looks gruesome,' said Rohan.

'Well, at least she had the decency to follow the dress code,' Maya replied.

'OMG, Janice Liew has been murdered. It's up to you guys to find the culprit who committed this heinous crime. In groups of three to five people, you'll need to move from one checkpoint to the next to uncover clues and solve this MURDER,' said Murali dramatically. 'Here's your first clue: This. Is. SPARTA! Good luck and may the best team win.'

'Wait, what?' Mei said, looking confused.

'I think that's a clue, which tells us where we need to go. The location of our first checkpoint,' Rohan clarified.

'This is Sparta? Isn't that a line from that Gerard Butler movie, *300*?' Maya asked.

'Haven't seen it,' confessed Mei.

'It's basically a heroic story about how a battalion of three hundred Spartan soldiers took on a large Persian army,' Rohan explained.

'Wait, I think I know where we're supposed to go.' Maya then led the way to their first checkpoint.

* * *

'The auditorium?' Mei asked doubtfully.

'Yeah, it's the only venue on campus that can hold a class of three hundred students,' Maya explained.

'Makes sense. I think we're the first ones here. Let's go in and check it out,' Rohan said as he pushed open the auditorium door. As Maya had guessed, the auditorium was indeed the right place. Right next to the podium, where Mr Ranjith usually stood to deliver his lectures, was a booth manned by two flapper girls.

'Welcome to the first checkpoint,' said one of the girls, who wore her hair in a cute bob.

'Love your outfits by the way,' the other girl, who had long, jet black hair and a feathery headband, beamed at the trio.

'Thanks, but we're the only ones dressed up. It's a little embarrassing actually,' Maya replied sheepishly.

'Seriously? I told Joshua to emphasize that this is a themed event. He never listens to me, that idiot,' Short Bob exclaimed. Looking at the shocked expressions around her, she regained her composure and added, 'Sorry about that. You guys look lovely.'

'Okay, moving on . . . before we give you your next clue . . .' Jet Black Hair started, before unveiling a bowl of steaming noodles from under the podium, '. . . you'll need to complete the spicy ramen challenge.'

'Oh, I've seen this on TikTok,' Rohan laughed. 'Is that the Korean Samyang noodles?'

'Yeah, it's suuuper spicy. One of you has to finish this bowl of ramen in under two minutes,' explained Short Bob.

Maya immediately turned to Mei, 'Babe, you've got this!'

Mei nodded with a knowing smile. She handed over her boa and cigarette holder to Rohan, stepped forward and picked up the chopsticks. The timer started and she inhaled the ramen at top speed. In five mouthfuls, she had devoured the noodles and had moved on to the spicy soup. She discarded the soup spoon and raised the bowl to her mouth. Exactly at the one-minute mark, she slurped up the last bit of soup and won the challenge.

'Damn, girl. That was impressive,' exclaimed Jet Black Hair as she handed them an envelope containing their next clue. For the rest of the night, they ran across campus from one checkpoint to the next, crushing every challenge that stood in their way. From choreographing a thirty-second dance number to playing Pictionary, they were on fire!

As soon as they got their final clue, they raced back to the foyer area, but there was another group hot on their heels. The girls ran as fast as they could, but their flapper dresses were not designed for sprinting. Finally, the other group reached the finish line before them and cracked the case wide open.

'We have our winners. Congratulations!' Murali announced just as the trio caught up, panting and totally out of breath.

'Fuckkk!' Mei cursed, louder than she probably should have. Everyone turned to look at them.

'What she meant to say was congrats,' Maya stepped in to do damage control.

'Yeah . . . congrats . . . well done,' Mei muttered unconvincingly.

'Anyway . . . help yourselves to some refreshments, guys. We'll wait for the other teams before moving on to the prize-giving,' Murali replied before heading to the stage to check on the prizes.

'Let's just go,' said Mei.

'But the refreshments look good!' Rohan protested. 'Look they have karipap, kuih, those fancy sandwiches, and mocktails.'

'I'm pretty hungry too, actually,' Maya added.

'Fine. Let's grab some food and get out of here.'

The other teams began trickling in and before long, Murali took to the stage to announce the winners.

'Welcome back, everyone. Without any further ado, let's call the winners on to the stage. Congratulations to Jeremy Chan, Alice Pang, and Gunaselan Murugan.'

This announcement was followed by a weak applause. Most of the teams that just arrived were distracted by the refreshments. The winners made their way on to the stage and received a huge fake cheque for the amount of 500 Ringgit. They posed as the campus photographer took their picture.

'All right, let's move on to the next one. The prize for best-dressed team goes to . . . Maya Joseph, Chong Mei Li, and Rohan Das!'

The three of them were busy snacking away and were caught totally off guard by Murali's announcement. They ditched their paper plates and cups and hurriedly made their way to the stage. To their surprise, they too were given a huge fake cheque for 250 Ringgit.

'Thank you for taking the effort to dress up tonight. You guys look amazing!' Murali added.

'You sure do, M,' Rohan whispered into Maya's ear. She smiled coyly as the campus photographer captured the moment. Just as Maya predicted, it was a night they would never forget.

Chapter 25

And just like that, they attended seven campus events, including an outdoor yoga class, Holi night, the annual rave, and an interactive Disney-inspired musical. Most of them were a hit, except for the 'Dining in the Dark' experience hosted by Foodie Inc., Maestro's newest club. The event ultimately involved a lot of poking and prodding in the dark and not much eating. Regardless, Maya considered Project 21-cum-8 Events a success thus far. The last event of the semester, the Maestro Ball, was coming up soon. It was an annual event organized by the student council and they usually pulled out all the stops.

This year, the theme was 'Glitz & Glamor: Old Hollywood Royalty.' Rohan and Maya were going together, while Mei was flying solo as usual. It wasn't that Mei wasn't getting asked out. In fact, she was—left, right, and centre! But no one quite caught her fancy and Mei was above caving to social expectations. She was happy flying solo and going to the ball with her best mates. Rohan left the task of picking what he would wear to Maya and Mei. He wasn't quite sure what the theme meant fashion-wise, so he was relieved to not have to think about it too much.

Maya and Mei, on the other hand, were beyond excited. Maya decided to channel her inner Marilyn Monroe with a figure-hugging, gold sequinned dress. She borrowed Mei's feather boa and draped it over her arms for the big night.

Mei decided to make a fashion statement, as usual. Instead of going for a red carpet-esque dress, she went for a perfectly tailored, black pantsuit. She was going to roll up the sleeves for a more dramatic look and pair it with a bejewelled cane. 'I can already picture the whole look in my head. I'm gonna do a bold red lip and wear dramatic drop earrings to tie it all together,' said Mei as they ate lunch together in the café.

'That sounds epic, babe. You're going to look gorgeous,' Maya replied.

'Mei, how much did your pantsuit cost exactly?' Rohan asked. Maya kicked his shin under the table and he winced. He saw it coming, but just couldn't help himself.

'Well, I would tell you, but then you'd have a heart attack, or worse, you'd lecture me about the value of money. My dad already does that, so I don't need you piling on as well, thank you very much,' Mei replied defensively.

'Okay, okay, relax. I don't know why you're getting so worked up about this. It's just a uni event, not the Oscars,' Rohan teased.

'A fashion influencer never misses a photo op. It might not be the Oscars, but it's being held at a five-star hotel and I heard they're actually rolling out a red carpet.'

'Babe, I'm sure you're gonna get some sick pics for the gram. Oh, Rohan, I almost forgot, I found the perfect rental suit for you,' Maya said, her eyes gleaming with excitement.

'Great! Can't wait to see it.'

* * *

Finally, it was the night of the ball. Maya and Mei started getting ready hours before the event. Meanwhile, Rohan threw on his suit fifteen minutes before they left. He met the girls downstairs by the pool. They were all decked up for the night. Rohan's jaw dropped when he saw Maya.

'Wow! You look gorgeous, M,' he said.

'Thanks, babe. You look very dashing yourself,' replied Maya as she admired Rohan's glamorous appearance. He wore a jet black suit with a red velvet bow tie and a matching pocket square. His usually messy hair had been tamed with gel and combed back, giving Rohan a very sleek look.

'Stand together, lovebirds. Let me take a picture of you two,' said Mei as she gestured for Rohan to stand next to Maya. Instinctively, Rohan came over and put an arm around Maya's waist. Maya couldn't help herself and she leaned in to kiss Rohan on the cheek. Just as she did, she heard the 'click' of Mei's camera.

'Perfect shot for the gram,' she said before sharing the picture in their WhatsApp group.

They made their way to the campus entrance, Maya holding Rohan's arm to steady herself as she teetered in her stilettos, and took a Grab car to the venue of the ball: Sonic Spa & Resort, a five-star hotel in the heart of KL. As they entered the hotel lobby, Maya and her friends were greeted by a jolly doorman who directed them upstairs to the Level 5 Ballroom.

'Oh-em-gee,' was all Maya could get out as she walked in and looked around the ballroom in awe.

The ballroom was an extravagant space that had over sixty round tables for guests and a large stage area right at the front. The ceiling was dotted with beautiful crystal chandeliers and the tables were set with silk tablecloths, gleaming plates, silver cutlery and vases of exotic, fresh flowers. Between the stage and the tables was an open area which she guessed would be used as a dance floor later in the evening. The ballroom was slowly filling up with students and buzzing with excitement. Waiters moved swiftly through the ballroom setting tables and serving drinks.

They walked over to their table and settled down. Soon after, a waiter served them sparkling apple juice. They sat at the table, enjoying the ambience of the ballroom while munching on the light snacks put out on their table. Once the ballroom filled up, the emcee kickstarted the event. The energy in the room was unlike anything Maya had ever experienced. She figured that this was how celebrities attending red carpet events must feel— extremely posh, excited and buzzing with adrenaline.

The stage was occupied with act after act, from singers to dancers and magicians. As they were entertained by top-class performances, the waiters served a variety of delicious dishes, including asparagus soup, grilled quail with roast potatoes, oven-baked seabass with seasonal veggies, an interesting palette cleanser and finally, a decadent chocolate mousse topped with fresh berries and edible gold flakes.

After dessert, the three musketeers headed to the photo booth right outside the ballroom to take some pictures. The photo booth had a plush, red velvet background and there were plenty of props to choose from.

Rohan picked a sign that read 'I'm with Ms Gorgeous'. Maya smiled coyly as she read the sign and gave him another peck on the cheek before picking up a sign that read 'Back off, this stud is mine!' Mei chose the comically oversized sunglasses and they posed with their props as the photographer took their pictures.

Just then, they heard the emcee announce, 'All right, this one's for all you couples in the audience tonight. It's slow dance time. Bring your other half to the dance floor and dance the night away.'

'Guys, that's your cue,' said Mei.

'No way. We'll wait for the open dance floor and go together,' replied Rohan. Maya smiled and looked over at Rohan affectionately. She loved how Rohan always looked out for Mei, never wanting her to feel like a third wheel.

'When will you guys ever get to dress up and slow dance like this again? This whole night feels like a dream. Please go and dance. I'll be fine. I'm gonna walk around and take pictures for Insta, yo.'

'Are you sure, Mei?' Maya asked.

'Yes, now go already,' Mei shooed them into the ballroom.

'All right, let's do this,' Rohan said as he took Maya's hand and headed to the dance floor.

* * *

Rohan and Maya slow danced in each other's arms as the song 'Perfect' by Ed Sheeran played in the background.

'This night has been wild. They really nailed the glitz and glamour part,' said Maya. The music was loud so she had to lean forward and speak into Rohan's ear. The sensation of Maya's warm breath on his cheek made Rohan tingle. The enticing smell of her perfume was driving him crazy as well. It was all he could do to not kiss her right there and then.

'Yeah, I don't think I've ever been to a hotel as fancy as this before,' Rohan replied, trying to distract himself from Maya's inviting lips.

'Me too. I can't believe we're leaving Maestro soon. Uni life has been . . . incredible.'

'It really has been. But whatever comes next, we'll take it on together, right?' Rohan looked into Maya's eyes longingly. She met his gaze and smiled coyly. How did he end up being so lucky? He was with the most beautiful girl in the room.

'For sure. I can already picture it in my mind. You at your fancy finance job, me writing away as usual, us at a cute little place somewhere in the city,' Maya replied as she gently lay her head on Rohan's chest and sighed in contentment. Oddly, Maya felt Rohan's body tense a little.

'Yeah . . . M, when you say city . . . where exactly do you picture us staying?' Rohan asked hesitantly.

'Here, lah, where else?' Maya laughed at what she thought was a joke, but quickly realized that Rohan was being quite serious. 'Wait, where do you picture us ending up?' she raised her head from Rohan's chest and looked up at him.

'Er . . . I don't know . . . I was thinking maybe we could spend some time in Delhi,' replied Rohan, treading cautiously.

Maya was speechless. They were so caught up with assignments, exams, and other things that they never got around to discussing their future. It was finally dawning on Maya that their time together at Maestro was coming to an end and they would have to figure out what to do next.

'Oh,' was all she could get out in that moment. She took a step back and froze, staring into the distance.

'It's just that I've spent the last few years away from home and I really miss it. My sisters are growing up so fast and I wanna be around, you know?' Rohan added.

'Uh-huh.'

'I didn't mean to spring this on you—'

'Rohan, can we please talk about this later?'

'Yeah, okay,' Rohan replied. They stood awkwardly in front of each other in silence as 'You Are the Reason' by Calum Scott started to play in the background. Rohan wanted to forget about the future and live in the moment. He wanted to draw Maya close, look into her eyes, and tell her he loved her.

Instead, he went against his better judgement and asked, 'But . . . what do you think?' He wanted to let it go, but he was too curious for his own good.

'Rohan . . .' Maya just wasn't ready to have this conversation.

'We're just talking, okay? Nothing's set in stone,' Rohan persisted.

Maya sighed. 'Look, I get that you miss home, but I don't see myself moving to India. I don't speak the language and I don't know anyone there.'

'You know me.'

'I don't know anyone apart from you,' Maya corrected, crossing her arms defensively.

'Okay,' Rohan instantly regretted bringing up the topic.

'We'll talk more later, okay?'

Rohan nodded in agreement. They tried to push this lingering issue aside and enjoy the rest of the evening. They put their arms around each other and gently swayed to the music, but the energy between them had changed. The excitement from before was gone; tension and anxiety had taken its place. An awkward silence fell upon them and soon, the slow songs switched to fast-paced dance music.

All the couples disengaged and more people started flooding the dance floor. Mei ran up to them and practically shouted to be heard over the loud music. 'Come on, time to partayyy!'

She grabbed Maya by the hand and directed them to the middle of the dance floor before jumping up and down with her hands in the air.

Maya didn't feel like dancing, but she didn't want to ruin Mei's night. She guessed Rohan probably felt the same way. She started dancing and so did Rohan. They danced for what seemed like ages. It was well after midnight when the DJ signed off and everyone cheered loudly for him. Exhausted from the eventful evening, the three of them booked a Grab and made their way back to Maestro. With Mei seated in the middle, Rohan and Maya felt more distant than ever before.

Chapter 26

Two weeks later, things got pretty bad between Maya and Rohan. As usual, Mei got caught in the crossfire.

'You guys are still fighting? Just talk it out and make up already,' Mei pleaded desperately as she barged into Maya's room and fell onto her bed.

Maya, who was sitting at her desk, watching a movie to distract herself, heaved a heavy sigh. 'It's not that simple, Mei. This is the worst fight we've ever had. Whenever we try to talk about it, things just get worse.' She swivelled around to face Mei, bringing her knees up to her chest and hugging them tightly.

'All this 'cos you guys can't agree on where to stay after graduation?'

'Yeah, it's a big deal, Mei. I can't just uproot my whole life and follow my boyfriend to India, and he refuses to accept any jobs here, even though he's getting offers. I don't know what to do.'

'Well, maybe you guys can do long distance for a while. He can find work there, you can stay here and write. There's FaceTime—'

'I can't have a relationship over FaceTime, Mei. We can't really be there for each other . . . we'll miss too much. It's a ticking time bomb, babe.'

'Okay . . . why don't you guys live in Delhi for a few years and then move to KL? By then, Rohan's sisters should be off to college and his family will be more or less settled. Then you can relocate here, have babies, dogs . . . whatever you two weirdos are into.'

'Hmm . . . I don't know, Mei. A few years can easily turn into a decade and before you know it, moving to KL is completely out of the picture . . . that's sort of what happened to my mum. My parents had plans to move to London after a few years, but something always came up and it never happened.'

'Maybe Rohan can work here? And once you guys are settled, he can always bring his parents over,' Mei suggested. She tried desperately to mend things between Maya and Rohan, but with each passing day, the frustration within her only grew.

'Yeah, I suggested that too. Rohan said his parents are too proud to come to Malaysia to live with him.'

Mei sighed deeply and replied, 'Well, you guys have to figure out some sort of compromise. I'm sick of being caught in the middle.'

'Mei, I'm going through a crisis right now. I can't just speed things along for your sake. Honestly, I can't believe how selfish you're being right now,' Maya retorted, starting to get a little annoyed.

'Selfish? Are you kidding me?' Mei grabbed her phone and after a few swift taps, Maya heard her phone ping on the table.

'Are you texting me? Seriously?' Maya snapped, her annoyance beginning to grow. She picked up her phone and opened the WhatsApp message Mei had sent her. It was a link to a fashion blog. 'Mei, I don't have time for dumb articles right now. If you haven't noticed, my life is kind of falling apart at the moment,' Maya lashed out.

'Yeah, 'cos it's always about your life and all your stupid drama, right? If you had bothered to open the link I sent you, you'd know that I was featured in "Beauty Queen", one of the leading fashion blogs in Southeast Asia. In terms of exposure, this is huge. I've been sitting on this for a week now and it's not the first time I've had to hide good news because of some stupid fight between you two. It has always been about you, you, you, isn't it? I'm not just a sidekick in the Maya Show, you know? I've worked hard and I deserve to celebrate with my best friends. But somehow whenever the two of you fight, it's as if I disappear into the background. For the past two weeks, you guys have been going on and on about your problems. It's all you can talk about. Do you realize you haven't once asked about my life ever since the ball?'

Maya was taken aback by Mei's outburst. She opened her mouth to respond, but no words came out. It was almost as if the conversation between them was lagging like in a bad Skype call. As she processed what Mei had said with a dumbfounded expression on her face, something clicked.

'Wait . . . Rohan talked to you about us? What did he say?' Maya asked eagerly, eyes wide, leaning forward towards Mei to know more.

'That's what you got from what I said? How fucking dense are you? You know what, I can't take this shit any more!'

By the time Maya could get a word in, Mei had stormed out of the room, slamming the door behind her. Not knowing what to do, Maya looked down at her phone and clicked on the link Mei had sent her.

It redirected her to a blog article entitled 'The Top 7 Malaysian Fashion Influencers to Watch This Year!' Maya scrolled down and at number five was Mei with a stunning picture of her in her signature pantsuit at the Maestro Ball. Under the picture was the caption, *Fashion is a lot like friendships. People come and go, but your besties are for life. Fashion trends come and go, but a well-tailored pantsuit never goes out of style!*

Maya's heart sank. She had no idea. Immediately, she closed her browser and opened Instagram. The 'Totally Mei' page had hit a record 500K followers and Mei's latest post was a picture of the three of them all dressed up for the ball: *Honoured to be featured on the iconic Beauty Queen blog this week. Thank you to my besties, Maya and Rohan, for not letting me give up on myself! #carveyourownpathtoglory #mybestiesarebetterthanyours*

Maya's eyes pricked with tears as she read the caption. Mei's Instagram page was her baby, and this was a huge milestone. A milestone that she couldn't share with either of her best friends.

Maya felt sick to her stomach. *How could I have been so blind?*

* * *

The following day was the last day of class before the start of their study break. Throughout her programme, Maya had had four electives to complete. Unlike other students who signed up for fun arts classes, Maya's electives were a mix of economics subjects that she took with Mei and Rohan.

For her final semester, she signed up for international economics and trade as her last elective. The subject was pretty dry thanks to the monotonous lectures delivered by Professor Patrick James. He was a visiting Professor from the UK, and the three musketeers had had the misfortune of landing him as their lecturer.

Dull as his classes were, Maya couldn't help but feel sentimental about that particular class. It was their last class together. And to make matters worse, none of them were talking to each other. Maya and Rohan had awkwardly taken their seats, leaving a space in between for Mei. However, Mei came in five minutes late, walked right past them and took a seat at the back of the class instead.

Rohan looked at Maya curiously, but she just shrugged, not wanting to get into the messy details with him.

PJs (the nickname bestowed upon boring Professor Patrick by the class) did a last-minute review of important topics for the finals. Maya took down notes, but she had a very hard time concentrating on what PJs was saying. Fighting with both your best friends will have that effect on you. Finally, PJs put an end to their misery, dismissing the class and wishing them all the best for their final exams. Mei swung her bag over her shoulder and left the room through the back door without giving Maya and Rohan a second glance. Maya hastily packed her things and raced after Mei.

'Mei, hold up. We need to talk,' Maya said as she chased after her surprisingly quick-on-her-feet bestie.

Mei pivoted around on her heels and bluntly replied, 'What do you want?'

'I just want to talk. Please,' Maya pleaded.

Mei turned away and continued speed walking. Maya took that as a signal to follow her and tried her hardest to keep up. After an intense walk, they reached their dorm unit. Mei unlocked the front door, tossed her things onto the dining table, and spun around to face Maya again, her arms folded antagonistically.

'Mei . . . I'm so sorry. I've been so caught up in my own drama that I had no idea what was going on with you. You were featured in "Beauty Queen!" And your account blew up big time. Those are huge achievements that I didn't even ask about or acknowledge. You even tagged me in your appreciation post, and it just flew right over my head. I'm so sorry, Mei,' Maya said before bursting into tears.

Seeing her best friend earnestly apologize and weep, Mei started to soften. 'I know you guys have been going through a rough time. And I want to be there for you, but . . . I'm battling some demons of my own, you know? The semester is coming to an end, and I have to make some tough decisions soon. I have no idea what I'm going to do. Do I take over my family business or do I keep doing this fashion thing? I'm so conflicted and I just felt like I couldn't talk to you guys.'

Hesitantly, Maya took a step closer to Mei and reached for her hand. 'Mei, look at how far you've come. Your account, the brand deals, you did it all on your own. You built something from scratch, just like you said you would. You've gotta stick with fashion. It's your thing, babe. It's what you were meant to do.'

Mei lunged forward and hugged Maya, almost knocking her off her feet. As she did, a dam within her broke and the tears, which she had been holding back for so long, started to flow. She simply cried and cried while Maya just hugged her silently, offering her a shoulder to lean on; something she had failed to do as a friend recently.

Never again, she promised herself.

Chapter 27

Maya and Mei had patched things up between them and it felt like things were back to normal, but not quite. For the rest of the study break, Maya and Rohan decided to hit pause on their argument and focus on preparing for the finals. The three musketeers were back to their usual study break routine: long hours of studying in the twenty-four-hour study rooms on campus, taking coffee breaks in between to stay alert and focused.

Things weren't exactly like they used to be, though. There was tension in the air, stolen glances at one another and awkward silences, but they knew that they had to buck up and prepare for the finals. As stressed as they were, the gang tried to savour their last few days as Maestro students. After late-night study sessions, they often strolled around campus, sipping on vending machine coffee, reminiscing about their fondest memories at Maestro.

'Remember when we threw you into the pool?' Mei asked on one particular night.

'How can I forget? Not exactly the birthday surprise I was expecting,' Maya replied.

'Well, it was fun for us. In fact, it seems like a nice night for another dip in the pool, don't you think, Mei?' Rohan teased.

'Don't you dare!' Maya warned.

'Ooh, yeah! We didn't get to take a picture last time,' said Mei menacingly as she closed in on Maya.

'You guys suck,' Maya practically yelled as she dodged Mei's advance.

As they walked back to their dorm rooms that night, Maya thought back on her birthday wish, desperately wanting it to come true.

* * *

Three weeks later, they were sitting for their final paper: international economics and trade. As usual, going through past year papers had helped a lot. After two and a half hours later, they were done. Leaving the exam hall was bittersweet for Maya. She felt like a huge weight had been lifted off her shoulders only to be replaced with a sinking feeling in the pit of her stomach. Exams were over, which meant that their time in Maestro was coming to an end. Worse still, there was no more putting off the argument with Rohan. They had to settle things once and for all. Just the thought of it sent chills down Maya's spine unlike any exam she had ever sat for.

The three of them discussed the final paper as they walked towards the dorm café. They ordered their usual nasi lemak and frappés before settling down at a table outside by the pool. They ate in silence, not knowing how to cope with this sudden end to their university life. The usual post-exam bliss was dampened by a weird sense of melancholy. The café's nasi lemak and frappés that they usually enjoyed, suddenly tasted bland and brought them little joy.

'So . . . what are you going to do, Mei?' Maya asked, breaking the silence.

'I'm going to . . . stick with fashion. My sister, Sue, is studying business as well. We had a long chat the other day and we have some ideas on how to outsource certain parts of production and distribution to make running the family business easier for my parents. Sue doesn't mind taking on a more active role in overseeing everything, but she made it clear that she doesn't intend to work herself to the bone like our parents did. Don't work hard, work smart, she keeps reminding me.'

'Dude, that's awesome! I never knew Sue had an interest in the family business,' replied Rohan.

'Yeah, I was pretty shocked too. She actually has some pretty good ideas. It's such a pity actually. All these years, my parents underestimated her without realizing she has a good head for business. Sue even suggested a possible future collaboration where we team up to offer closet makeovers. She would remodel the closet space and I would come in to fill the closet with looks matching the client's criteria and style,' Mei explained excitedly.

In all their time in Maestro, Maya had never heard Mei speak of Sue so fondly.

'Actually, that's a great idea. You could call it "Totally Mei & Sue". I would definitely book a makeover with you guys,' Maya gushed. 'You Chong sisters really have a knack for business, lah!'

Mei smiled and modestly replied, 'Well, let's not get ahead of ourselves. It's not going to be an easy road ahead. Convincing my parents to hand over the reins to Sue will be another battle altogether, but, hey, at least we're a united front, right?' After some thought, she picked up her phone from the table and added, 'Let me just check whether "Totally Mei & Sue" is taken.'

Later that night, Mei had a dinner date with one of her influencer friends, and Maya and Rohan were left with a rather large elephant in the room to deal with.

* * *

Rohan suggested that the two of them go out for dinner somewhere nice as it had been ages since they last went out on a date together. They agreed not to talk about their tricky conundrum, at least not until the end of the night. After an exhausting few weeks, they just wanted to relax and reconnect before diving into a potentially heavy and loaded conversation.

At half past seven, they took a Grab car to Sawadikap Delights, a popular Thai place nearby. Maya wore a white, off-shoulder maxi dress that accentuated her beautiful collar bone. She paired that with a rose gold choker necklace that Rohan had given her for her twenty-first birthday. Rohan, meanwhile, opted for dark slacks and a denim jacket over a grey T-shirt. He wore one of his dressier sneakers for the occasion.

In the car, they browsed through the menu available online and discussed what combination of dishes to order. Both being foodies, they wanted to go through the menu thoroughly, cross-checking Google reviews for recommendations, and walk into the restaurant prepared. Since they had done their homework, ordering was a breeze. They nabbed a nice, quiet table in a corner before the restaurant started filling up.

Within fifteen minutes, their food was served. The jasmine rice, green curry with chicken and eggplant, seafood tom yum and stir-fried morning glory all looked mouth-wateringly delicious. They dug in and after a lot of oohs and aahs, all the plates were soon wiped clean. To complement the spiciness of the tom yum, they ordered a cool red ruby dessert with crunchy water chestnuts, sweet jackfruit, coconut milk, and crushed ice. Throughout dinner, they talked about all the events they had attended over the semester. They both agreed that the murder mystery night was the most memorable.

'You seriously looked like you were going to clobber Mei,' said Rohan.

'Can you blame me? She convinced us that it was a costume party and we ended up walking into the place like we had just stepped out of a time machine,' Maya defended.

'Regardless, you looked beautiful as always,' Rohan added as he gazed adoringly at Maya.

Maya smiled coyly, averting her gaze and calling for the waiter to refill their drinks. It had been over a month since their rift began, since Maya heard such loving words from Rohan. She was nervous about how the night would go, but she tried her best to live in the moment and savour Rohan's company.

They talked and laughed a lot that night, more than they had in a long time. Neither of them wanted the night to end. They ate their red ruby dessert so slowly that, after some time, one of the waiters politely asked them whether they were done because there were other customers waiting to be seated. After quickly paying for their meal, they were back in a car, heading to Maestro. The ride back was filled with a tense and awkward silence. They knew what was coming and neither of them wanted to face it.

Maya suggested that they take a walk around campus to clear their heads. The campus was pretty much dead. They walked around for a bit and then decided to sit in the open field and do some star gazing. Rohan chivalrously took off his denim jacket and laid it on the grass to protect Maya's white dress. They sat down and looked up at the beautiful night sky filled with twinkling stars. Stars that were lightyears away felt so close, but the distance between Malaysia and India was somehow too much to bear. The irony dawned on Maya, and she wondered whether Rohan was thinking the same thing.

Rohan sighed and said, 'What are we going to do, M?'

'Honestly . . . I have no idea,' Maya replied. After a couple of weeks of blissfully ignoring their problems, they were back at square one.

'M . . . did you think about my suggestion?' Rohan asked hesitantly.

'You mean the one where I uproot my whole life and move to Delhi with you?' Maya answered, failing to hide her irritation.

'No, the one where you realize I left home for three years and return the favour,' Rohan shot back.

'You do realize that I left home too, right? Perhaps *you* can "return the favour" and move to Penang?' Maya knew it was ridiculous, but she was lashing out in frustration. They had had these arguments and gotten stuck in these loops of endless bickering before. Nothing had changed.

'Fine. What do you suggest we do?' Rohan asked.

'I think we should stay here in KL. You've gotten job offers here, and there are plenty of writing opportunities for me as well. Whenever we miss home, we can fly back to see our families.' Maya looked pleadingly at Rohan as he considered her idea with a pensive expression on his face.

'Flight tickets aren't cheap, M. Staying in KL will cost us a bomb and I don't think flying all over the place is gonna be possible. Your plan sounds good on paper, but it's not practical,' Rohan retorted bluntly after giving it some thought.

'Well, if I move to Delhi, I'll have the exact same problem, right? I won't be able to fly back to Malaysia very often. I don't speak the local language, I don't know anyone else there, I'd feel so isolated.'

Rohan met Maya's gaze and looked into her eyes, desperately trying to make her understand his point of view. 'M, I'm from Delhi and I speak fluent English. If you work at a publishing house over there, your colleagues will speak English and you can make new friends. I didn't know anyone when I first moved here either.'

'Rohan . . . I'm sorry you miss home and all, but you chose to be here, right? Why do you have to punish me for that? You make it sound like I forced you to come here. News flash, you came here 'cos you wanted to. You've gotta stop guilt-tripping me to move to Delhi with you,' Maya snapped, once again failing to conceal her growing frustration.

'What the hell? I'm not guilt-tripping you, okay? Delhi is a nice place and I think you'd like it there. I was looking online and there are any number of publishing houses you could work with. My distant cousin's an editor and I could introduce you to him—'

'Babe, I know you mean well, but the idea of moving to another country to be with someone you're dating is kinda crazy. What if we break up? What if things just don't work out? It would be different if we were married.'

'Are you telling me you wanna get married?' Rohan asked, utterly shocked.

'Of course not! Neither of us is ready for such a big step. We're only twenty-two, for God's sake. What I'm saying is . . . I can't come to Delhi, Rohan,' Maya said, feeling deflated.

'The solution can't be to stay here, far from both our families.'

'But we're here right now. We've been here for three years now. It feels like home to me. Why can't we try to make it work here?' Maya pleaded desperately. 'Just give it a year or two. If we can't make it work by then, we can think of some other solution.'

'I don't think a year or two will make any difference, M. Even if I don't like it here, you won't wanna move to Delhi—'

'But—'

'—and I might end up hating you for it. I don't want that to happen,' he said under his breath. Tears flowed unheeded down Rohan's face. Soon, Maya's eyes started to well up as well.

After another hour of back and forth, they were both emotionally drained and too exhausted to continue. They retired to their respective dorm rooms with no resolution in sight. It was a sleepless night for both of them.

Chapter 28

It was time to fly back home. Each in a different direction. Rohan was leaving for India in a week and the girls were heading home a week after that. They had made these travel plans much earlier in the semester to provide themselves ample time to pack their things, vacate their dorm rooms, and enjoy some post-exam bliss together for the last time. Instead, Rohan and Maya spent most of their time talking, desperate to find a solution to their problem, some sort of a middle ground that they could both agree on, but to no avail. Every discussion led to further arguments and misunderstandings. Mei gave them space and spent a lot of time hitting up local thrift stores, looking for vintage finds to feature on her Instagram page.

After a particularly heated argument, Rohan and Maya decided to cool off and give each other some space. Maya spent the day in her dorm room, going over every conversation, every argument she'd had with Rohan, beating herself up for all the stupid things she had said in the heat of the moment, things she would never ever be able to take back. The next day, Maya texted Rohan to meet her in the rooftop garden. Throughout their time in Maestro, the rooftop garden had always been a sanctuary for them, a safe haven to which they could retreat when things got overwhelming.

As Maya waited for Rohan, she sat on their usual bench and gazed out at the KL skyline. The skyscrapers, tall buildings, and distant mountains made for an incredible view.

How could Rohan not appreciate the beauty of this city? They had created so many beautiful memories there and it felt like a no-brainer to Maya to stay on in this vibrant city and build a life here together. A few moments later, the elevator doors opened, and Rohan walked over to the bench.

'Hey, you wanted to see me?' he asked awkwardly.

'Yeah, we've got to talk, Rohan. Please, sit down.'

Rohan sat down beside Maya and admired the view. 'I'm going to miss this view.'

Maya smiled. 'I was just thinking the same thing. You know, you don't have to say goodbye to this view. I know living in the city is expensive, but we could always find a small apartment on the outskirts for not very much. Whatever we save, whatever we can, we can send home to your family.'

'Maya, not this again. You're not going to convince me to abandon my family and move here for the bloody view.'

'So, it's okay for me to abandon my family?' Maya lashed back.

'You don't even like your dad. You'll just be leaving your mum and she can always come over and stay with us whenever she likes.'

Rohan's response left Maya more than a little stung. 'Wow, how long have you been waiting to throw that in my face?' She could feel her eyes welling up and her face turning red.

Seeing how hard his words had hit home, Rohan softened. 'Look, I didn't mean it that way. I just . . . I can't move here permanently, M. It would break my mother's heart.'

'I can't move to Delhi either, Rohan. My mum gave up her whole life moving over here for my dad. She left behind her family, her friends, everything she'd ever known. I've seen how hard that has been for her, how lonely and isolating it can be. Mum gave up everything for Appa, embraced his culture and learned to make his food the way he likes it, and I've never heard him say so much as a thank you to her. I can't do it, Rohan. I won't put myself through that,' Maya said adamantly.

'It won't be like that for us—' Rohan protested, trying to convince Maya that their story would be different, before she cut him off.

'You don't know that. Don't make promises you can't keep. I'm sure my dad promised the world to my mum. In the end, it came to nothing. He isn't the least bit interested in visiting her family back home despite knowing how homesick she gets. Things can change, Rohan. So don't tell me that it'll be different for us,' Maya retorted.

'So . . . what do we do?'

Silence fell upon them for what felt like an eternity. Neither of them wanted to voice out the inevitable truth, because once those words were spoken, they would become real. Finally, Maya broke the silence and said the words Rohan was dreading to hear, 'This relationship has an expiration date, doesn't it?'

As soon as she uttered those awful words, she could no longer contain the sadness that had built up within her. Tears streamed down her face and before long, she was sobbing. Rohan put his arm around her and Maya rested her head on his shoulder as she wept until she had no more tears left to shed.

As the sun set over their beloved city, they knew life would never be the same again.

* * *

'You guys broke up?' Esther asked, shocked. After their rooftop meeting and breakup, Maya was a mess. She spent all day crying in her room and as much as Mei tried to comfort her, it didn't seem to help at all, so she decided to call in reinforcements. When Mei called Esther and explained what had happened, she immediately drove down to Maestro and with Mei's help, snuck into Maya's dorm room. Esther took one look at Maya and knew things were bad. Her eyes were puffy from all the crying and she had massive dark circles like she hadn't slept for weeks. The usually bubbly and quick-to-lend-a-smile Maya looked utterly deflated. It broke her friends' hearts to see her like that.

Maya nodded in answer to Esther's question. She told them about the arguments, the breakup, everything.

'We were constantly arguing and just couldn't agree on anything. It's only been a few days and this has already created so much animosity between us. We don't want to end up hating each other, so we agreed that the best thing to do would be to . . .'

Maya couldn't bring herself to finish her sentence. They were done. YaRo was now a thing of the past. She couldn't believe it. How short-sighted they had been. Not once in the last two years did either of them stop to think about the future. They had been so busy basking in the light of their romance that they had completely ignored the fact that, eventually, the sun would set.

'Isn't there some way you guys could work things out?' Esther suggested hopefully.

'It's complicated . . . I don't want to move there, and he doesn't want to move here. What's the point of doing long-distance when, down the line, we're doomed to implode and fail?' Maya managed to squeeze out in between sobs. Esther and Mei didn't have an answer to this question, so they sat in sombre silence beside Maya on the floor, handing her tissues and stroking her back to comfort her. After some time, Esther remembered something her grandmother once told her that seemed relevant to Maya's predicament.

'You know, my grandma lives in China. We visit her every other year and we're always asking her to move here and stay with us. She often seems puzzled by the request as if we've suggested something completely ridiculous. For her, she can't understand why we'd want her to move away from her home. She says that she's been living in the same house, by the same river and mountains, her whole life, and when her time comes, she wants to look out at the river and mountains before passing on peacefully. When we tell her that we miss her, she smiles and says she misses us too, but she wouldn't ask us to move to China and stay with her because, then, we wouldn't be happy. She told us that, if you truly love someone, you want them to be happy, and sometimes . . . that means letting them go. Nainai makes it a point to call us regularly and even though she's a world away, I still feel her love and warmth . . . I'm sorry, I got carried away with that story. I don't know if it helps,' Esther ended.

'That's beautiful, Esther. Your grandma sounds like a really wise woman,' Maya replied with a weak smile.

'Maya . . . whatever you decide to do . . . we're here for you, okay?' Esther assured Maya.

'Yeah, no matter what happens, we'll always be here,' Mei added.

Maya put her arms around each of their shoulders and pulled them close for a group hug. This might be the week from hell, but at least she had two angels by her side. After a couple of hours, Mei walked Esther to her car and on the way back up, she packed some food from the dorm café. Maya needed to eat, although Mei knew Maya's appetite would be non-existent. Hopefully the aroma of her beloved nasi lemak ayam rempah would at least entice her to take a few bites. She headed upstairs and found Maya in bed, curled up into a ball. Mei forced Maya out of bed, got her to wash her tear-streaked face and urged her to eat. Maya gave Mei a tight hug and put up a strong front to reassure her friend.

'Thanks, Mei,' said Maya as she ushered Mei out of her room. 'Don't worry, I'll eat. I just need some rest. I'll see you tomorrow, okay?' she added before closing the door.

As Mei retreated to her room helplessly, Maya settled down on the floor and opened the nasi lemak packet that Mei had given her. Piping hot rice with spicy sambal and crispy fried chicken would usually make her mouth water, but just as Mei had predicted, Maya had no appetite. She took a few mouthfuls and set it aside before crawling into bed, pulling the comforter over her head. She wanted this nightmare to be over. Finally, she cried herself to sleep.

* * *

After a couple of depressing days spent crying in her room, the day Maya was dreading finally arrived. Rohan was checking out of the dorm and leaving for India. Maya could hardly wrap her head around it. She thought she had more time, but the hours and minutes had just slipped through her fingers. Maya already felt distanced from Rohan and they would soon be thousands of miles apart physically as well.

'How did we get here?' Maya asked herself for the umpteenth time. 'This was never part of the plan.'

Rohan had texted her a few times over the past couple of days, but she hadn't responded. She didn't know what to say. His last text from the night before nearly broke her heart.

* * *

I guess that's it then. I want to say goodbye, but it feels like you don't want to talk to me any more. Everything just feels so . . . final. You've always been true to your word, so I understand. We're officially broken up and that's that. Goodbye, M.

A few moments later, Maya's phone pinged again.

Whatever happens, don't stop writing.

Maya cried for hours after reading that message. Ultimately, she ran out of tears and just lay in bed, staring at the ceiling. Rohan's message and Esther's words swirled around in her head.

We're officially broken up and that's that.

She told us that, if you truly love someone, you want them to be happy, and sometimes . . . that means letting them go.

After some time, she dozed off. When she finally came to, she felt groggy and her head throbbed. She reached for her phone and was shocked to see that it was two o'clock in the afternoon. Rohan's flight was at half past three. Maya jumped out of bed, washed her face, and threw on a pair of jeans and a T-shirt before rushing out the door. She got into a Grab car and asked the driver to step on it. The airport was an hour away without traffic. Maya checked Google Maps and the jam was slowly starting to build up. She was cutting it close, real close.

Maya tried calling Rohan, but it went straight to voicemail. She tried Mei next, but there was no answer. She couldn't do anything but pray and plead for the driver to go faster.

'Miss, I'm going as fast as I can. If I go any faster, I'll get fined, lah,' the Grab driver exclaimed in response to Maya's constant nagging to hurry up.

Finally, with minutes to spare, they pulled up in front of the Kuala Lumpur International Airport departure lane. Maya paid the driver and ran inside as fast she could.

Chapter 29

FIFTEEN YEARS LATER

Maya sealed the two packages on the table in front of her. As she took a sip of her latte, she stopped to admire the beautiful leaf carefully drawn on her cuppa by the talented chef-cum-barista.

His latte art is improving, Maya thought to herself. As another patron entered the café, a gust of wind blew Maya's hair onto her face. She tucked her beautiful curly hair behind her ear and caught a glimpse of herself in her reflection in the glass front door. Thanks to a simple, yet effective, skincare routine introduced to her by none other than her fashionista best friend, Maya had a clear, beautiful complexion with no wrinkles even in her mid-thirties.

Just then, Maya's phone pinged. It was a text from Amanda, confirming the seating arrangements for the upcoming event.

Maya still couldn't believe it was actually happening. After all these years, her magnum opus was finally complete. She thought back to the time Susan Tan had hated her story as a novice writer and smiled. How times had changed.

Just then, a tall, well-built gentleman wearing a black apron walked over carrying a plate of cheesecake.

'Our new mixed berry cheesecake, on the house,' he said before setting the plate down in front of Maya. He flashed his signature pearly whites and sat down beside her.

'Thanks, Dustin. Your coffee art is getting better by the way. Your leaf looked like an actual leaf today, instead of a vague blob,' Maya teased as she took another sip of her latte.

Dustin laughed and replied, 'Thanks, I guess.'

Maya took a bite of the cheesecake and almost moaned. 'Oh my God, this is so good.'

'I know, right?' Dustin replied before producing a small fork from the pocket of his apron and helping himself to a bite of the cheesecake. Maya glared at him threateningly. 'Sorry, I couldn't help myself,' he said with a cheeky smile.

Reluctantly, Maya shared the cheesecake, but swiftly nabbed the last piece for herself. 'Sooo good,' she gushed as she put the morsel into her mouth, closing her eyes to shut out the world around her and savour the sweet and tangy flavour of the cheesecake.

'I'll let Mel know you liked it. She's an absolute wizard when it comes to baking. Thanks again for introducing us, Maya. Launching M + D has seriously been a dream come true. I wouldn't have been able to start a place of my own without Mel's expertise.'

'Dustin, stop thanking me, okay? I've known you guys a long time and it just made sense, you know? You're a great chef, she's a talented baker, you both wanted to open a restaurant in KL.

And what you guys have done here, this . . .' she gestured to the space around them, 'is amazing. I'm really happy for you, Dustin.'

A new customer walked into the café and Dustin excused himself to take her order. Maya sat back and looked around as she continued to enjoy her cuppa. The café was a modern space with white walls and floors, equipped with light brown wooden furniture. It oozed minimalistic charm, which reflected Mel and Dustin's combined sensibilities. The display case beside the counter showcased a variety of delectable pastries and cakes including their signature tiramisu tart, matcha red bean cake, tropical fruit tarts, and blueberry cream cheese Danish.

The menu overhead was equally impressive with a list of Dustin's specialities including salmon poke bowl, fried chicken sandwich, and chicken pesto pasta. M + D opened six months ago, and business was booming. 'Serve good food at a reasonable price and people will come,' Mel often told Dustin and she was right.

Maya finished her latte and packed up her things. She needed to stop at the courier on the way home to mail her packages.

As she headed out, she waved at Dustin and said, 'Send my love to Esther.'

'Will do, Maya,' he replied, flashing his pearly whites once again, before attempting a seahorse-inspired latte art for his customer.

* * *

It was a regular Thursday for Mei. She was sorting out inventory at her boutique in Singapore, 'Mei-be It's Time.' Wrap dresses were all the rage and they were practically flying off the racks. Mei made a mental note to order more dresses and matching accessories before the Christmas season. She was going through boxes at the back of the store when she heard the bell. She walked out of the back room and saw a courier boy standing at the cashier's counter, looking around the store curiously, taking in its eclectic décor.

The boutique oozed boho-chic vibes. The shelves lining the walls were filled with accessories like hats, bangles, earrings, and necklaces. In the centre of the boutique were garment racks carrying dresses, skirts, tops, and scarves. Each garment rack carried a specific colour in all its shades, creating a beautiful rainbow effect. To one side of the cashier's counter was a large, full-length mirror and on the other, a fitting room with the black velvet curtains drawn open.

One corner of the boutique boasted a hat rack with attractive pet collars in various designs and colours. Above the hat rack was a sign that read: 'Fur Finders. Making missing pets a thing of the past.' Sales were still going strong after all these years, especially online. Their Fur Finders had found their way to almost every corner of the world including North America, Europe, Australia, and Africa. Mei had since expanded their range of pet collars to include matching scarves and berets for pet owners who wished to colour coordinate with their beloved furry friends. While Mei wanted to give a share of the profits to her fellow co-founders, her friends refused, insisting that Mei was doing all the heavy lifting, so it was only fair that she keep all the profits.

'Sorry to keep you waiting. We're a little short-handed today,' said Mei, walking over to the counter. He snapped out of his reverie and smiled earnestly. 'No worries. I've got a package here for Chong Mei Li.'

'Yep, that's me.' Mei signed the necessary forms and as the courier boy left, she eyed the package curiously. The moment she spotted the Malaysian postal stamp on the other side, she had a pretty good idea who it was from. She ripped open the brown paper packaging and found a rather thick hardcover book within. The front cover was stunning. It featured an illustration of planet Earth against a black backdrop, with shimmering stars and galaxies in the distance. Above this illustration, in bold font, were the words:

MISSION EARTH

by

Maya Joseph

A wide grin on her face, Mei extracted her phone from her back pocket and opened WhatsApp. She clicked on one of the pinned contacts on the top and hit call.

'Heyyy!'

'I just got your book. The cover looks gorgeous, babe,' raved Mei.

'Thank you! I still can't believe this is happening. You're coming to the book launch, right?' Maya asked nervously.

'Of course, lah! There's no way I'd miss it.'

'Okay, good. I'm freakin' nervous and I need my bestie there.'

'Babe, you have nothing to be nervous about. You had me hooked right to the end and I'm not even a sci-fi person. You've written an amazing book, Maya. People are gonna love it,' Mei said confidently.

'I hope so. By the way, what am I gonna wear?'

'Well, as your bestie-slash-stylist, I've prepared a very smart, very sleek, yellow pantsuit for you.'

'You just love your pantsuits, don't you?' Maya teased, thinking back on the glamorous pantsuit Mei wore to the Maestro Ball way back when.

'As I always say, they never go out of style. Don't worry, I'm gonna have you looking fabulous for the launch.'

'I know you will. All right, babe, I've got to go. Message me your flight details later. I'll come pick you up.'

'Okay, see you soon.'

Just as Mei was heading back to continue with the inventory, she received an incoming call from her sister, Sue.

'Hey, what's up?'

'Mei, I've got good news,' Sue said so excitedly that she was almost squealing.

'Wait, do you mean . . .'

'Uh-huh. I just heard back from the investors. They really liked our pitch and want to go forward with the partnership.'

'Oh my God . . . that's amazing. What did they say?' Mei practically squealed too.

'They said they want us to test the waters in Malaysia first, but they think our business has the potential to expand to Singapore, Hong Kong, and Taiwan in the next few years.'

As Sue shared more details, Mei's eyes began to well up. 'I can't believe it. After so many years of trying to make this work, it's actually happening.'

'I hate to say I told you so—'

'Then don't.'

'You know I have to. I told you things would work out.'

Mei smiled to herself and shook her head. Sisters, no matter how old, will always be sisters.

'You were right. Thanks to you, "Totally Mei & Sue" is actually going to happen.'

'I can't wait to tell Papa the good news.'

'Me too. I'm coming to Malaysia in a few days. Maya's book launch is on the 25th and I'll fly in to KK (Kota Kinabalu) after that. Let's break the news together, okay?'

'Sounds good. I'll email you the contract the investors sent over. Check it out and we'll discuss it when you get here, ya?'

'Okay, talk soon, sis. Bye.'

Mei returned to work with a spring in her step. She was on cloud nine and even the dull task of sorting through inventory couldn't bring her down.

* * *

Rohan reached for his bedside table and turned off his alarm before it even rang, not wanting the sound to wake his wife. His biological clock invariably woke him up at the same time every day, 5.25 a.m. He got out of bed as quietly as he could and made his way to the bathroom. Rohan was still slim, his hair as messy as always, but his once jet black hair was now dusted with strands of grey, giving him a sophisticated salt-and-pepper look. His once carefree face was now etched with lines that gave his age away. He had a few creases on his forehead and crow's feet near his eyes. It was a working day and Rohan would have to leave for the bank soon. He wore a blue long-sleeved shirt tucked into black trousers, his usual office attire.

He got dressed and leaned over the bed to kiss his wife goodbye. She stirred in her sleep and her eyes fluttered open. Even half asleep, she looked beautiful, Rohan thought to himself. She smiled and gave him a peck on his cheek before dozing off again. Rohan gently closed the door behind him and left for office. The traffic wasn't too bad this early in the morning. As he drove down the streets of the city, he could see street vendors setting up their stalls for the day. Even at this hour, customers were trickling in to get breakfast before the start of their working day.

Within twenty minutes, Rohan had pulled up in front of ABC International Bank. As branch manager, he was usually one of the first to arrive every morning. The security guard, stationed at the front entrance, opened the door and greeted Rohan. Rohan walked past the bank's waiting area to the back, where his cabin was located. He set his backpack down and got to work. He was checking the transaction reports from the previous day as the other employees began trickling into the branch.

By 8.00 a.m., the tellers and bank officers were at their stations, all set for the day ahead. The guard flipped the sign hanging on the front door over and the bank was officially open. Soon, the branch was filled with customers. It was a busy day, as usual, for all of them, including Rohan. He attended to a few technical problems faced by the bank officers, signed off on some large transactions, and spoke to a few chatty customers about their new products, all before lunchtime.

At noon, he headed out for a quick lunch. He walked across the street and ordered a plate of fried noodles at a roadside stall. The owner greeted Rohan and served his regular customer with a warm smile. Rohan enjoyed his simple yet satisfying lunch and washed it down with a nice, hot cup of coffee. Within twenty minutes, he was back at his desk. Rohan didn't like going off on long lunch breaks. He was always nervous about leaving his staff, just in case they needed his help with some emergency.

Afternoons were especially busy, and time just flew by. Soon it was 5.00 p.m., and once again, the guard flipped the sign on the front door over, closing the bank for the day. The tellers and officers tallied their transactions and cash, before printing out the necessary reports for Rohan. Once everything was settled, Rohan headed home. He was tired, but the thought of going home to his family put a smile on his face. By 7.00 p.m., he was back home. As he got out of his car, he saw his wife at the door. She greeted him with a loving embrace and Rohan planted a kiss on her forehead.

'TGIF,' Rohan said, excited to welcome the weekend.

'I wish I could celebrate too, but I've still got one last chapter to finish,' his wife groaned.

'Tell you what, why don't you take a break tonight and finish that chapter tomorrow? We can watch that new rom-com you've been meaning to catch on Netflix.'

'As long as you promise not to doze off midway through the movie.'

'I'll try my best,' Rohan said with a wink. Even as a thirty-something, he still had that boyish charm.

'All right, go wash up first. I've made naan and butter chicken for dinner.'

Rohan happily went upstairs to get changed. He'd never admit this out loud, but he preferred his wife's butter chicken to his mum's—a fact that he will take to the grave.

* * *

Rohan stood on his open terrace overlooking the city the next day as he sipped on his morning cup of chai. Delhi buzzed with the sounds of traffic, the occasional car horns, and the voices of street vendors promoting their products. He smiled as he listened to this morning orchestra. Somehow, the sounds of the city made his chai taste that much more satisfying. As he finished his cuppa, his wife joined him on the terrace.

'Rohan, there's a package for you.'

'For me? Who's it from?'

'No idea. It's pretty heavy though.' She handed him the package and took the empty cup from his hand. She watched as he ripped the brown packaging paper to reveal a book inside.

'Oh my God,' Rohan slipped the book out of the wrapping and turned it over to examine the front cover.

MISSION EARTH
by
Maya Joseph

He opened the book and on the first page was a familiar picture. A much younger Rohan was beaming back at him. He was standing beside Maya and Mei. It was the picture taken during the Murder Mystery Night back in Maestro. Below the picture were the words:

This book is dedicated to my friends, Mei Li and Rohan Das, who believed in me even when I refused to believe in myself.

'She did it. She actually did it,' he exclaimed in amazement.

'Is that you? Wow! Look at you guys, all dressed up,' his wife said excitedly, looking at the picture of her husband and his buddies.

Rohan chuckled. 'Yeah, this was taken ages ago, back in uni. This is Mei and this is Maya.'

'Oh, so *this* is the Maya you told me about?' she teased.

'Yeah, I guess she must have gotten our address from Mei.' As he flipped through the pages, an envelope fell to the ground. Rohan picked it up and opened it. There was a handwritten note, an invitation, and a flight ticket inside. The note read:

Without you, there would be no book launch to celebrate. I need to thank you in person, my dear friend. For old time's sake, would you hop on a plane and come see me in KL?
M

The artsy flyer provided all the details of the event:

Join us as the beloved Malaysian author Maya Joseph
launches her debut novel!

Renowned for her short stories and poetry, Maya has made
a name for herself as quite the storyteller. To date, she has
churned out over 100 short stories and 25 poems.

Everest Publication cordially invites you to this young star's
book launch party!

Venue: Sonic Resort & Spa, Event Hall II
Date: 25 September 2034
Time: 3 p.m. onwards
Dress code is smart casual.
See you there!

Stapled to the invite was a first-class plane ticket to KL with
Rohan's name on it.

'You know you've got to go for this thing, right?' Rohan's
wife pointed out.

Rohan looked at her in astonishment. 'Are you sure,
Pooja?' Flying to another country to meet an ex-girlfriend isn't
something most wives would be thrilled about.

Pooja smiled. 'You talk about your uni days all the time. I
know she's your ex, but I also know that she and Mei were good
friends to you. I think this trip would be good for you, Rohan.'

Rohan pulled his wife in for a warm embrace. 'You're really
something else, you know that? Every time I think I've got you

all figured out, you turn around and surprise me,' he said before planting a kiss on her forehead. What he really wanted to do was kiss her passionately on the lips, but they were standing on the open terrace and there was a good chance that their conservative neighbours might catch a glimpse of what they were up to. And then the gossip would be endless!

'All right, I've got to go and study. Your wife isn't going to get her master's degree if she keeps slacking, you know?'

Rohan threw his head back and laughed. 'You? Slacking? No chance. Go on then, finish that last chapter. I'll bring you some nice hot coffee in a bit.'

Pooja threw caution to the wind and pulled her husband in for a kiss. Just then, a little four-year old with pigtails came running to them.

'Daddy, pick me up.' Rohan swept her up and spun her around. 'Faster, Daddy, faster,' the little girl shrieked and her father happily obliged.

Chapter 30

Rohan gathered his things and left his hotel room. It was exactly half past two and he needed to get to the event by three o'clock. He rushed down and got into a Grab car. Initially, Rohan thought he'd book a room at Sonic Resort, but got a shock when he looked up the room rates online. The cheapest rooms cost 400 Ringgit a night. Being a banker and a family man, Rohan had grown to be very thrifty, and he couldn't bring himself to spend that kind of money, so he booked a room at a nearby hotel for a fraction of the price.

When the car pulled up in front of Sonic Resort, Rohan quickly made his way to Event Hall II. He opened the giant doors into a spacious room that was only slightly smaller than the ballroom where the Maestro ball had been held fifteen years ago. There were rows of chairs arranged to face the stage, which had a podium on one side and three plush, red velvet armchairs on the other. In the background, there was a large banner that featured the cover of Maya's book along with big, bold words that read:

MISSION EARTH
A Sci-Fi Novel by Maya Joseph
Official Book Launch

The stage was empty but for a technician who was setting up a mic for the podium. The front row was occupied by the press. Rohan could tell they were media people from their lanyards and all the camera equipment. The next fifteen rows or so were filled with people Rohan didn't recognize. He looked around, hoping to see a familiar face somewhere. Then, he heard someone behind him.

'Rohan, you came.'

Rohan spun around. 'Oh my God, Mei. It's so good to see you,' he swooped in for a hug.

Mei looked like she hadn't aged at all. She had flawless skin, not a wrinkle in sight. Her hair was long and straight and her outfit was as impeccable as always. Suddenly, Rohan felt a tad underdressed in his jeans, white T-shirt, and chequered shirt.

Mei sensed Rohan's discomfort and couldn't help but laugh. 'Some things never change.'

'The invitation said: "smart casual". I thought this passed as smart casual.'

'Well, it's leaning more towards casual, but I'm happy to see you, so I'll let it slide. Come on, I see Uncle Joseph and the others. Let's go sit with them.'

They made their way to the fourth row, where they had a good view of the stage. Rohan had never met Uncle Joseph before, having only seen pictures of him, but he recognized Maya's father. His hair had turned grey, and his skin was beginning to sag, giving him a rather haggard appearance. He broke into a wide smile when he saw Mei and got up to greet her with a hug.

'Hello, my dear. It's been so long. How are you?'

'Hi, Uncle, I'm good. I want to introduce you to someone. This is Rohan,' Mei replied, gesturing to the tall, awkward man standing behind her.

'Hello, it's nice to meet you. How do you know Maya?' Uncle Joseph asked, extending his hand towards Rohan.

'We were . . . friends back in uni,' Rohan replied awkwardly as he shook Uncle Joseph's hand.

'Oh, that's nice. Thank you for coming to Maya's book launch. I'm sure she'll be happy to see you.'

Just then, Rohan noticed that there were two other familiar faces beside Uncle Joseph. 'Dustin, Esther! How are you guys? It's been ages since I saw you two.' It had been over a decade, but Rohan could recognize Dustin's signature pearly whites from a mile away. They sat down and the old friends began to catch up.

'You guys are engaged? That's amazing.'

'Yeah, we met on campus in Cyberjaya and really hit it off,' Esther replied.

A few minutes later, three women entered the event hall through the side door beside the stage and the crowd erupted into a thunderous applause. They made their way to the stage. Two of them sat down while the other walked over to the podium to address the crowd. Rohan smiled to himself as he saw Maya sit down in a chic, yellow pantsuit.

'Welcome, everyone. Thank you so much for coming to this special event. Today, we're here to celebrate the launch of Maya Joseph's debut book . . .'

The woman, who Rohan later found out was Everest Publication's head of marketing, Amanda Pang, went on to talk about Maya's career as a prolific writer of short stories and listed all the awards she had won over the years. Listening to this,

Rohan beamed with pride. He always knew Maya was destined to be a writer.

'. . . now, let me introduce our guest of honour, Maya's friend and mentor, to say a few words. Let's welcome the one and only Susan Tan.'

Wait, what? Rohan was in utter shock as he watched the woman sitting beside Maya, whom he hadn't noticed before, stand up and walk over to the podium. It was Susan freakin' Tan. Maya's arch-enemy back at Maestro, on stage, to say a few words at her book launch. Rohan couldn't wrap his head around it. The world had gone mad.

'Bro, wipe that shocked expression off your face. They're friends now,' Mei said, trying hard not to laugh. Rohan straightened up and tried to hide his shock.

Susan had a stern expression as she reached the podium and adjusted the mic. She then shifted her gaze to the audience and her expression mellowed into a smile.

'Ladies and gentlemen, you all know Maya Joseph as a talented writer who weaves humour and humanity into her stories. But I knew her long before she became a renowned writer.' Susan spoke slowly and her voice was soft, but she had the full attention of the audience. The cameras were flashing as members of the press took pictures of Susan, but she wasn't fazed. This wasn't her first rodeo. One doesn't become a beloved national literary treasure without getting some media training along the way.

'As a young adult, she took my writing 101 class at Maestro University. I hate to admit it, but I once told this talented woman to stop writing. Told her, to her face, that she didn't have what it takes to be a writer. In fact, the book we're launching today is based on one of the first short stories she ever submitted in my class. I gave that eager, hopeful girl a bad grade and little guidance on what she could do to improve. At the time, I thought I was doing her a favour, saving her from the sometimes cut-throat literary industry. Needless to say, we didn't part on good terms . . .' Susan turned to look at Maya, smiling.

'But a few years ago, she approached me at a literary conference. To be frank, I was not too keen to face her. What surprised me was that she didn't rub her success in my face. She took my hand, looked me in the eye and thanked me. She said I had motivated her to keep writing, to keep getting better, so that one day, she could prove me wrong.' Susan laughed lightly as she reminisced about that day.

'Since then, we've developed a friendship and although Maya would have you believe that I'm her mentor, she's the one who taught me a very valuable lesson about what it means to be a good writer. When you believe in your story with a fierce conviction and pour your heart into it, great things can happen. Ladies and gentlemen, let's give it up for Maya Joseph.'

The audience erupted into applause yet again. Mei and Rohan cheered loudly as Maya walked over to the podium. She embraced Susan and moved over to the mic.

'Hello, everyone. Thank you for being here . . .'

After an hour, Maya had given a heartwarming speech and had also read an excerpt from her book. Rohan was overloaded with new information from Maya's speech and was still processing everything. A few years ago, Maya's mother had passed away from cancer and since then, Maya and her father had grown quite close. In fact, Uncle Joseph was clapping louder than anyone else in the room when Maya was called to the podium and he was listening intently, his eyes brimming with tears and pride during the reading.

After Maya's speech and book reading, Amanda Pang thanked the audience for coming and asked everyone to head

over to the adjoining room for some light refreshments. A few
people headed out, but most of the attendees stuck around to
congratulate Maya. Rohan felt awkward about interrupting, so
he sat down with his uni mates, chatting with them until, one by
one, everyone else left and it was just them and Maya left inside.

'Babe, you were amazing up there,' Mei ran over to Maya
and hugged her.

'God, I was so nervous.'

'You were incredible, Maya,' Uncle Joseph said, holding
his daughter's face in his hands and kissed her forehead. 'Your
mother would've been so proud, my dear.'

'Thank you, Appa,' Maya replied, her eyes brimming
with tears.

'Yeah, you were amazing, M.' Mei and Uncle Joseph stepped
aside, revealing Rohan behind them, standing awkwardly, not
knowing what to do next.

'Rohan, you came,' Maya exclaimed and hugged him with
such force that he almost fell backwards.

'Of course I came! Wouldn't have missed it for the world.'

Dustin and Esther congratulated Maya and after a round
of hugs and excitement, Mei chimed in. 'You guys catch
up, we'll go check out the refreshments.' She ushered the
others out, giving Rohan and Maya a chance to catch up after
all these years.

'I can't believe you actually dedicated the book to us.'

Maya laughed. 'Well, I made you guys a promise, and I
meant it.'

'M, your book . . . it's incredible.'

'You read it?' Maya asked excitedly. Even after all these
years, the thought of Rohan reading her story still brought
her joy.

'Of course. I couldn't put it down; I finished it in two days.'

'You always were a fast reader.'

'Well, I liked your story even back then, M. I told you it was good.'

'Yeah, yeah, you were right.' Maya rolled her eyes, and continued, 'Now let's sit, these heels are killing me!' They sat down in the last row and Maya kicked off her shoes. 'That's better,' she said with a sigh of relief.

'I'll never understand why you girls torture yourselves like this. Pooja does the exact same thing. She wears high heels and by the end of the evening, she ends up walking barefoot.'

'Pooja . . . she's your wife, right?' Maya asked awkwardly.

'Yeah . . . M, I'm sorry I didn't invite you to the wedding. I didn't know if you'd—'

Rohan was taken aback when Maya threw her head back and laughed heartily. 'Who invites their exes to their wedding? That would be super awkward.'

'I guess you're right,' Rohan chuckled nervously.

'So how did you guys meet?'

'Oh, er . . . our parents set us up actually. Our dads are old friends.'

'That's nice. Mei said you guys have a kid?'

'Yeah. Her name's Anandhi.' His face lit up at the thought of his daughter. 'She turned four this year, but my God, she's so freaking smart. Kids these days pick things up so quickly.' He proceeded to open his phone gallery and show pictures of Anandhi to Maya.

'She's very cute. Thankfully, she looks like her mother,' Maya teased.

Rohan rolled his eyes. 'Yeah, yeah, whatever. She's a good kid.'

'You have a beautiful family, Rohan. I'm happy for you,' said Maya.

'Thanks, M. I guess we've both come a long way since Maestro, huh?'

'God, yeah. So much has happened, you know? Sometimes I wonder where all the time has gone. One day we're carefree uni students and the next we're adults in our thirties with jobs and families. It's crazy.'

'Yeah . . . I love my life, but sometimes I wish I could go back to those days, even for a little while.'

'We had some good times, didn't we?'

'We really did. Remember the murder mystery night?'

'And the ball?'

'Things were so . . . light and breezy back then.'

'Well, it did get kinda intense towards the end,' Maya said. 'You know, Rohan, I never told you this before, but the day you left for India . . . I was there at the airport.'

'Wait, what? Why didn't you come over and say something?' Rohan asked in shock.

'I was too late. By the time I got there, your flight had already taken off. I didn't know what to do . . . I thought I'd talk to you at graduation, but then you didn't come. I figured you didn't want to see me,' Maya revealed.

'I'm sorry, M . . . I didn't know. Why didn't you just call me?'

'I don't know . . . I guess I didn't know what to say.'

Rohan was reeling from shock. All this time, he never knew that Maya had followed him to the airport.

'Do you think . . . if you had caught up with me that day . . . things would be . . . different?'

Maya gave this question some thought and said, 'I don't know how things would have worked out. But if things were different . . . if I had forced you to move here away from your family or if you had compelled me to move to Delhi with you, we probably would have grown to resent each other over time. I'm glad that didn't happen, Rohan.'

'Me too, M.'

'It must have been a shock to Pooja to suddenly receive a package from me in the mail. I'm sorry if that caused any problems.'

'No, not at all. She knows all about you, about us. Actually, she's the one who encouraged me to come.'

'Wow, she sounds like a keeper,' Maya said, winking at Rohan.

'Yeah, she's really something,' he replied with a smile.

'Rohan . . . thanks for coming today. I know we haven't been in touch for a long time, but I really appreciate your being here.'

Rohan waved his hand dismissively. 'I'm happy to be here, M.'

'Actually, there's something I've always wanted to tell you.'

'What is it?' Rohan asked curiously.

'I wanted to say . . . thank you. Back in uni, when I got bad feedback from Susan, I told you I wanted to quit writing and you encouraged me to stick with it. If it weren't for you, I would have given up a long time ago.'

'M, I honestly didn't do anything—'

'You did way more than you realize, Rohan, and I never thanked you for it. We may have had our problems, but you were always a great friend. Thank you for everything.'

Rohan's lips curved into a smile as he got misty-eyed. 'You were a great friend too, M.' Maya gave his hand a gentle squeeze. 'I mean, you introduced me to the wonders of nasi lemak. I practically owe you my life,' he continued, a smug grin on his face. Maya laughed and slapped Rohan's hand.

Just then, Mei walked back into the event hall. 'You guys all right?' she asked, sounding concerned.

'Yeah, we're fine,' Rohan replied.

'Good. Babe, the event was great and all, but the refreshments suck. Let's get out of here and go to Dustin's café.'

'Dustin has a café now?' Rohan asked curiously. The surprises just kept coming.

'Yeah, it's a pretty nice place near here,' Maya replied.

'Wow!' said Rohan. He was surrounded by friends who knew their calling and just went for it. Maya with her writing, Mei with her fashion empire, and Dustin with his love for food. Rohan had grown to like his role at the bank, but he wasn't madly passionate about it. It put food on the table and allowed his family to have a comfortable life. He had no regrets, but he vowed to dedicate more time to painting, a newfound hobby, when he got home. If there was one thing this amazing bunch of people had taught him, it was to follow one's passion.

'Dustin's coffee art is so much better than before, Mei,' Maya said, snapping Rohan out of his reverie.

'No coffee. I won't be able to sleep tonight,' Rohan replied.

Maya chuckled. 'He makes pretty good hot chocolate as well. I've just got to say some goodbyes and then we can go,' Maya sprang out of her chair and headed into the next room.

'All right. I'll call Dustin and let him know we're coming,' Mei replied. Before long, they were all huddled together in the back seat of a Grab car, heading over to M + D Café. 'So, you don't drink coffee after 5 p.m.? You've become such an old man,' Mei teased.

'Hey, there's nothing wrong with that. Do you see this salt 'n' pepper situation I've got going on?' Rohan said, pointing at his messy hair. 'The ladies love it.'

Mei and Maya looked at each other and burst out laughing. 'Dude, what ladies? It's been fifteen years and you're still stuck with us,' Maya retorted.

At the café, they were greeted by Dustin and Esther who had reserved a table by the window for them. They ordered a round of drinks, which Dustin had prepared specially for them, showcasing his impressive coffee and hot chocolate art. They also ordered some cakes, including Mel's mixed berry cheesecake, from the display case, and settled down for a nice chat. The five of them sipped on their hot drinks and indulged in delicious cakes while talking about anything and everything. There was so much catching up to do and it was always great to be in the company of old friends.

In a couple of hours, they would go their separate ways.

Rohan back to India on a night flight; Mei off to Sabah the next day to see her sister; Maya on the North-South Highway with her dad, heading home to Penang; Dustin and Esther staying behind in KL. But in that café, for that moment in time, they were back to being the Maestro gang, teasing each other, swapping stories, and laughing louder than they ever had before. It's funny how some things never change.

Acknowledgments

I wouldn't have been able to write this book without the help of so many amazing people. Thank you to Nora Nazerene from Penguin Random House SEA for giving me the opportunity to share this story, which is close to my heart, with all of you.

Thank you to the amazing team of editors at Penguin Random House SEA who worked tirelessly to help me tell this story. They challenged me and pushed me to do better at every turn, teaching me countless lessons along the way. Special thanks to Thatchaayanie Renganathan, Surina Jain, and Usha Surampudi. Editors are unsung heroes who help writers put their best foot forward, operating on the sidelines, expecting no credit for themselves. The work you do is incredible and I can't imagine writing this book without your support. From the bottom of my heart, thank you.

I also want to take this opportunity to thank the design team at Penguin Randon House SEA. When I submitted my manuscript, I was asked what my vision for the front cover was. Not only did the design team honour this vision, they exceeded all my expectations. They've created a cover illustration that brings Maya, Rohan, and Mei to life and for that, I am eternally grateful to them. Special thanks to Adviata Vats.

Writing a book is incredibly satisfying, but it can also be challenging at times. There have been instances when I almost gave up on our three musketeers and their story, but the support of my family and friends kept me going. Amma and appa, thank you for everything. You've always been there for me through all the ups and downs. A lifetime isn't enough to repay you for all that you've done. I hope I make you proud. Thank you to my friends, Kala, Nisha, and Preetha, who have encouraged me endlessly since the very beginning.

I also want to thank my furry friend, Patchi, for keeping me company as I wrote this book. Whenever I felt stuck or overwhelmed, he was always there to cheer me up with cuddles and a good ol' game of fetch.

Most importantly, I want to thank my husband, Karthig. Without you, there would be no book. You've known Maya, Rohan, and Mei as long as I have, and even when I was ready to give up on them, you weren't. Thank you for supporting me throughout the process of writing this book. Now that the book is finished, shall we kick back and order frappés for two? Love you always, for all your days, till end of time.